The
PHANTOM
SHERIFF

Center Point
Large Print

Also by Walker A. Tompkins and available from Center Point Large Print:

Deadhorse Express

This Large Print Book carries the Seal of Approval of N.A.V.H.

The
PHANTOM
SHERIFF

Walker A. Tompkins

CENTER POINT LARGE PRINT
THORNDIKE, MAINE

This Center Point Large Print edition
is published in the year 2017 by arrangement with
Golden West Literary Agency.

First US edition: Phoenix Press

The text of this Large Print edition is unabridged.
In other aspects, this book may vary
from the original edition.
Printed in the United States of America
on permanent paper.
Set in 16-point Times New Roman type.

ISBN: 978-1-68324-522-3 (hardcover)
ISBN: 978-1-68324-526-1 (paperback)

Library of Congress Cataloging-in-Publication Data

Names: Tompkins, Walker A., author.
Title: The phantom sheriff / Walker A. Tompkins.
Description: Center Point Large Print edition. | Thorndike, Maine :
    Center Point Large Print, 2017.
Identifiers: LCCN 2017024773| ISBN 9781683245223 (hardcover : alk.
paper) | ISBN 9781683245261 (pbk. : alk. paper)
Subjects: LCSH: Large type books. | GSAFD: Western stories.
Classification: LCC PS3539.O3897 P47 2017 | DDC 813/.54—dc23
LC record available at https://lccn.loc.gov/2017024773

To J. C. ALLISON,
who, hunting headlines down El Paso way,
stopped a border guerilla's bullet and bled
printer's ink; who badgered Pancho Villa
in his den and lived to tell the tale—
for you, old Unk, I tell this tale!

The
PHANTOM
SHERIFF

CHAPTER I.

Thundering six-guns broke the siesta stillness in Smoketree. Dozing cowboys reared erect in tilted chairs on the saloon porches lining the shady side of the street. Boots slogged out of the Border State Bank, thudding an offbeat to the deadly rhythm of the shots.

Two masked men, carrying a loaded gunny sack between them, bolted across the wooden sidewalk, vaulted a cottonwood hitch bar and sprinted for the horses which a Mexican confederate was watering at a public trough in midstreet.

From the unused store building alongside the bank came another whipcrack of shots. The swart Mex pitched dead from his saddle, losing his grip on the bridle reins of the ponies.

With snorts of panic, the three horses galloped up the dusty street toward the cactus forest of Whispering Desert, beyond the outskirts of the little Arizona town.

Yells of dismay came from the two bank robbers thus caught without means of making a getaway. But only for an instant did they remain standing in the thick dust of the wheel-rutted street.

Already, bullets were kicking up little gray

geysers about their chap-clad legs, from the gunman stationed inside the Long Trail Mercantile building.

The owl-hooters dropped their plunder-laden gunny sack and ran for the protection of a row of freight wagons lined up in front of a livery barn across the street from the Border State Bank.

Not until the shooting from within the store building ceased, indicating that the two desperadoes had reached the canvas-hooded wagon boxes, did the cow-town residents appear to break out of their trance.

Chairs clattered as onlookers of the shooting fracas fled through batwing doors for the protection of saloon walls. Three Mexican *ninos*, playing in the mud around the horse trough, fled screaming into an alleyway.

Then a deadly silence blanketed the town like a pall of doom.

"Try to leave them wagons an' you'll get shot to pieces!" roared an authoritative voice from inside the broken windows of the store. "The best thing for you lobos to do is toss out yore hardware an' step high an' handsome out into the open with yore hands up!"

Men tensed at the sound of that voice. It belonged to hard-shooting old Buck Clawson, sheriff of Smoketree. They divined a reason back of the veteran tin-star's hiding inside the long-deserted walls of the store building.

It looked as if old Clawson had been expecting the bank robbery. Too full of bandit savvy to station himself inside the Border State Bank—a ramshackle one-room affair which afforded no hiding place for an armed guard—the grizzled old sheriff must have lain in wait for the robbers at a point inside the Long Trail store where the punched-out windows would command a view of the bank lobby nearby.

Onlookers who had seen Clawson's bullets pepper to the ground around the escaping bandits' legs were sorry that the old sheriff's aim wasn't what it used to be.

An ambusher's slug had plowed a furrow through the sheriff's scalp not a month before, and the shock had done something to Clawson's nerves. His hands, once rock-steady, now quivered like those of a man with palsy.

No lawman, no matter if he was as game as a bayed panther, could hope to ramrod a tough cow-town like Smoketree if he couldn't put bullets somewhere near the target. In all probability the shot that had dumped the Mexican confederate had been pure luck.

For a long minute no sound came from the bandits who had scurried inside the prairie wagons in front of the livery stable.

Then Sheriff Buck Clawson yelled again, his

voice reechoing from the false fronts on the shady side of the street:

"Yuh wonderin' how come I knowed you was goin' to pull a stick-up today?"

The town shivered, waiting for the bandits to reply.

"Well, a greaser over at Gila Jack Shadmer's saloon got too much mescal Saturday night an' did some talkin'!" roared Clawson, from somewhere inside the store building. "He told me yore names. Pete Cameron o' Bisbee, an' Les Padillo o' Lordsburg. An' both of you was figgerin' on makin' a split with Gila Jack, because he arranged the stick-up!"

Of one accord the eyes of the hidden watchers of the halted gun battle swiveled down-street toward the Lucky Dollars Saloon, owned by the chief of Smoketree's outlaw element—Gila Jack Shadmer, gambler and ranch owner.

Even as they looked, the slatted doors of the Lucky Dollars swung open to reveal the tall massive figure of Shadmer himself.

Clad in his black frock coat in spite of the heat of the Arizona summer sun, Shadmer looked the part of the gambling dandy he was. Sunlight winked off a diamond-studded horseshoe pin in his silk cravat; glittered from the gold-plated studs adorning his gun belts and the leather band of his flat-crowned Stetson.

Leaning against a porch post of his saloon,

Shadmer took a black cheroot from his vest pocket and casually bit off the end with gold-capped teeth.

"If you're so sure them bank robbers are wearin' my collar, why don't you smoke 'em out of them wagons, sheriff?" called the gambler. "You're the law in this burg, ain't you? You could have tallied 'em both inside the bank if your trigger fingers didn't shiver like a tumble-weed in a cyclone."

A torrent of profanity issued from the sheriff's hide-out inside the Long Trail building. Shadmer imagined that he heard throaty jeers from the outlaws hidden there in the freight wagon.

And then a new sound entered the electric tension that had jelled Smoketree. The drumming of hoofbeats, and a cowboy's voice lifted in carefree song:

"I'm jest a driftin' waddy,
  But I shore am plenty proddy,
    An' I come from old Wyomin':

I can ride an' rope an' shoot,
  An' use my fists to boot,
    But what I like the best is roamin'!"

Sheriff Clawson, peering out on the sun-drenched street from the vantage spot where he crouched with trembling six-guns covering the

13

freight wagon opposite, scowled as he caught sight of a lone rider emerging from the sahuaros and smoketrees at the rim of the town.

Trailing behind the rider's lather-soaked roan were two bay ponies—those belonging to Pete Cameron and Les Padillo, the bank bandits. Hackamore ropes led from the two riderless horses and were dallied about the cowboy's saddlehorn.

Men held their breath in suspense as the rider slowed his bronc to a walk and stopped singing. He halted directly between the Long Trail store and the innocent-appearing freight wagons.

"Howdy!" yelled the stranger, shoving a gray sombrero back from sweat-sopped hair and peering up and down the street. "Ain't anybody home in this mangy cow-town?"

No one answered the man's yell, although half a hundred eyes were trained on him.

They appraised a lanky youth barely past voting age, his grinning face tanned to the color of ginger by sun and wind. He wore a red-checkered shirt and cactus-scuffed chaps of chocolate-brown bullhide, and there were long Montana-style spurs on the kangaroo boots.

A brace of bone-stocked Colt .45s rode the rider's thighs, and the walnut butt of a Winchester saddle gun projected from a boot under the right saddle skirt. But his hands were piled on saddlehorn, well away from his shooting irons.

"I know *somebody* lives in this God-forsaken, prairie-dog village!" yelled the newcomer again. "Because three broncs rattled their hocks out o' here just as I was driftin' in. I managed to sling a rope on these two, but the other one cut into the cactus."

Nothing but echo responded to the rider's words.

"Whoever belongs to these crow-baits," warned the cowboy, undaunted by his strange reception, "had better come out an' claim 'em, or I'll sure as heck turn 'em over to the nearest tannin' factory!"

Sheriff Clawson relaxed. The stranger's words proved that he was not a fourth member of the holdup gang. His bedroll and provision-stuffed saddlebags ticketed him for a drifting cowpoke who had blundered into a gun-fight unawares. The intervening horse trough had kept the waddy from spotting the dead Mexican.

Gila Jack Shadmer, still leaning against the porch post of the Lucky Dollars Saloon, raised a voice in answer to the cowboy's hail:

"Better tie those nags to the wheel o' one o' those prairie schooners an' then burn horse hair out o' town, stranger. You ain't settin' your saddle in a very healthy spot, right now."

The cowboy hipped over in the cantle and let slitted brown eyes range along the false fronts until he spotted Shadmer.

15

"Meanin' what? Not that I doubt what you say about this burg bein' plumb unhealthy. It looks like a graveyard with roofs, from where I set. I'm a stranger in these parts. Name's Spook Sidlaw, and I nev—"

A spear of flame lanced through a knothole in one of the prairie wagon's boxes a few feet away. Timed with the savage roar of a six-gun, the Wyoming ranny felt his horse rear aloft with a snort of agony.

Then, its spine severed by a bullet, the cow pony collapsed in a heap in the middle of the street.

CHAPTER II.

A second slug ripped out of the wagon box to singe the sleeve of Spook Sidlaw's red-checkered shirt, even as the startled cowhand kicked boots free of tapaderoed stirrups and leaped away from his toppling mount in time to save himself a fractured shin.

Only for an instant did the man from Wyoming remain in a standing position. He had no idea where the mysterious bullets came from, for the bandit's guns was exhausting its fumes inside the canvas-hooded freighter.

But of one thing Sidlaw was positive—somehow or other he had blundered into a hot spot, and to remain there another second would be inviting sure death from bushwacker's lead.

"Run for it, cowboy!" came a hoarse yell from the abandoned store building. "Either hightail it, or drop flat!"

Sidlaw started running, his eyes making a circuit of the street opposite, searching for the owner of the warning voice.

The nearest point of vantage was the broken-down old store building directly opposite. He headed in that direction, drawing his bone-stocked Colts as he ran.

Then he caught sight of a pair of gun barrels

resting on the weather-pealed window sill. Veering sharply to the right, the sprinting cowboy groaned as he saw orange flames spurt from the six-shooters.

But the bullets were not aimed at him. He heard them slap into the hickory wagon spokes on the prairie schooners alongside his dead horse.

Immediately to the right of the store building was a bank. But it was too far away to offer refuge and would necessitate recrossing the line of fire in order to reach it. To the left was a saloon, its windows framing white, frightened faces.

"Reckon that's the spot for me!" gasped Sidlaw as he did a kangaroo hop to the wooden-awninged porch. "Leastwise, no shootin' is comin' from there."

The green bat-wing doors slammed open before Spook Sidlaw's driving shoulders, and he slid to a halt on the sawdust-sprinkled floor, glaring about him in the subdued light.

One sweeping glance of the interior of the barroom told its mute story. Men, frozen in attitudes of suspense, crouched at the windows which fronted the street.

"Will somebody tell me what in heck's going on out there?" demanded Sidlaw, holstering his guns and staring about him. "I reckon I was plumb mistaken when I sized up this town for not bein' on the lively side. I just lost a two-hundred-buck hoss out there!"

Men crowded respectfully aside to make room for the lanky Wyoming man as he went to a window and peered out.

Sidlaw was in time to see two men leap from one of the freight wagons. Shots rang out from the ramshackle store building once more, but the men dived safely behind the carcass of Sidlaw's fallen horse and lay still, momentarily safe.

Even as Sidlaw stared in puzzled disbelief, he saw a brown hand reach up over his dead horse and fumble at the hackamores tied around his saddlehorns.

"They're the jaspers who owned those runaway broncs, eh?" surmised the cowboy. "Must have dropped my horse so as to make sure their own nags would stay put where they needed 'em, near as I can make out."

He broke off with a startled oath as he perceived, for the first time, the corpse of the slain Mexican sprawled near the watering trough.

"An' that third hoss I couldn't rope out in the cactus must have belonged to that greaser—right?"

A slab-muscled man clad in a grimy bartender's apron, who stood at Sidlaw's elbow, grunted affirmatively.

"You got the set-up figgered correct, stranger. You like to got yourself a one-way ticket to hell when you dabbed your loop on them horses an' brought 'em back to town. They belonged to some yahoos who held up our bank next door."

Sidlaw whistled in amazement.

"The hombre in the store buildin' is Buck Clawson, our sheriff," went on the barkeeper. "He tallied the Mex who was holdin' the horses, an' the nags run out o' town before the other two *bandidos* could straddle 'em."

Sweat leaked from Spook Sidlaw's skin as he understood the death trap into which he had so innocently ridden.

"Those fellers who jumped out o' the wagon an' are hidin' behind my horse are the owl-hooters, eh? They aim to make a gitaway before the sheriff tallies one of 'em."

Even as he spoke, Sidlaw glanced back outside to see that the bayed outlaws had untied the hackamores of their runaway mounts and even now were pulling the two nervous horses closer to the dead saddler's carcass.

"Of all the loco tricks! I played right into their hands an' brought their ponies back to 'em!" groaned Sidlaw. "An' I lost my own top peg-pony in the bargain! I'm goin' to help that sheriff!"

Scowling angrily, Spook Sidlaw strode outdoors, guns drawn. His entrance on the scene prompted the two bandits to make flying leaps toward their saddles, gambling their lives

20

against the hidden sheriff's inability to steady his quivering hands long enough to draw a bead.

But it wasn't necessary for Spook Sidlaw to use his Colts.

Even as the two bank bandits reared into saddle, a burst of gunfire came from the Long Trail store building.

Squalling curses, Les Padillo tried to remain in the stirrups of his wildly bucking horse while he gripped his gun wrist with his left hand to steady it and poured slugs at the window where Sheriff Buck Clawson was crouching in gun smoke.

Spook Sidlaw, watching the brief melee, marveled that the trembly old lawman could shoot as well as he did.

Buck Clawson thumbed his Peacemakers in rapid succession. And luck, plus the fact that Les Padillo's horse was sunfishing violently, put the outlaw at a disadvantage.

Crimson gushed from Padillo's mouth as a bullet severed his jugular vein. His body bounced from the saddle like a sack of potatoes and was catapulted out of the stirrups to land in a jackknifed position over the rim of the horse trough, head and shoulders submerged in the slimy green water.

Another burst of firing and the hombre whom the sheriff had called Pete Cameron threw up his arms and toppled from the saddle, his lungs riddled with searing lead.

"Good goin,' sheriff!" congratulated Sidlaw under his breath.

With an oath of satisfaction, Sheriff Buck Clawson straddled the window sill of the Long Trail building and strode out into the sunshine, slowly holstering his Frontier model .45s.

Spook Sidlaw nodded his appreciation of the old lawman's victory as he watched Clawson walk slowly across the street. Buck was a typical sheriff of the old frontier school—white of hair, hands dyed saddle color by the suns and winds of sixty summers, but carrying his six feet four with a certain jauntiness that bespoke inner youth.

Crash!

From somewhere—no one in Smoketree town knew where—came the ear-numbing explosion of a Winchester .30-30.

Halted in midstride by the impact of a bullet tunneling his side, Sheriff Buck Clawson swayed, tried weakly to lift his guns, then buckled at the knees.

Shaking a palsied fist toward the Lucky Dollars Saloon, Clawson spoke in a voice that chilled Sidlaw's veins—gasping out words that Sidlaw was later to remember all too vividly:

"You . . . ambushed me, Gila Jack. But I reckon our score'll git squared up! The Phantom Sheriff . . . is on his way. Between us we'll tame this burg . . . an' wipe you off the map, Shadmer—"

Voice trailing off, Sheriff Clawson toppled forward, his face striking the adobe.

Spook Sidlaw's eyes raked up and down the street, searching for a tell-tale plume of smoke to reveal the dry-gulcher's position. He saw none. The lone gambler who had greeted him from the porch of the Lucky Dollars Saloon was no longer in sight.

Where the shot had come from, Sidlaw could not fathom. Its direction was lost, at least to his ears, in the confusing echoes hurled back by the false fronts of Smoketree's business houses. The bullet could have come from any one of fifty vantage points.

Behind him, Spook Sidlaw could hear angry voices commenting on the sheriff's ambush:

"Gila Jack done that, I'm bettin' my last chip!"

"Hell, yes! Didn't Clawson call his gunnies by name? Wasn't Clawson wise that they were figgerin' on holdin' up the Border Bank?"

"Better hobble yore lip, Dave. If Gila Jack Shadmer gets wind that you're accusin' him of gunnin' ol' Buck, you'll be roostin' in boothill before long. Shadmer's been honin' to ramrod Smoketree, an' with Clawson gone I reckon he's goin' to."

Sidlaw listened, and did not like what he heard. Whoever Gila Jack Shadmer was, it was obvious that Smoketree had him labeled as Clawson's assassin. Sidlaw had been in cow-country settlements before, and had seen men quail to the authority of a ruthless gun boss.

And then the stranger from Wyoming perceived that Sheriff Clawson was not dead, nor even unconscious. The game old lawman was trying to drag himself toward the jail house, half a block up the street.

"He needs help," muttered Sidlaw. "An' he's liable to draw another dry-gulch shot—"

Squaring his shoulders grimly, the Wyoming cowpoke headed out into the street toward the fallen sheriff.

CHAPTER III.

No shot pierced the silence as Spook Sidlaw stooped and picked up the gaunt old sheriff.

Carrying the wounded lawman as he might a child, the Wyoming saddle tramp headed up the street to where he had detected a sun-warped sign reading:

JOS. FRAZER, M. D.
CORONER
MALPAIS COUNTY, ARIZONA

Clawson had slumped into unconsciousness by the time Spook Sidlaw carried his blood-dripping victim up to the doctor's office. The door opened to reveal a white-headed old cow-town medico, already rolling up his sleeves preparatory to working on the wounded patient.

"A dirty shame," panted Dr. Frazer, telling Sidlaw to lay Clawson on a sheeted couch. "It's a shame that he was cut down just when he'd dropped them two bank robbers. I hate for Marie to hear about this. It'll break the poor girl up plenty."

Sidlaw's face was clamped in harsh lines as he obeyed Frazer's bidding and brought a steaming teakettle of water from a kitchen range in the next room.

"Some jaspers talkin' just after the shootin' allowed they figgered a man name of Gila Jack Shadmer did this, doc."

Frazer, busy with shears as he snipped off the sheriff's blood-soaked shirt, looked up with a start.

"Listen, cowboy. You're a stranger here, else you wouldn't mention Gila Jack's name in the same breath with a murder. Better leave town, or if you stay, don't talk out o' turn. It ain't healthy—as our boothill can testify. Shadmer gun bosses Smoketree, an' if the sheriff here don't pull through—"

Sidlaw compressed his lips and went to a window. From the bank a cashier hurried out to reclaim the sack of loot which the bandits had been forced to drop in their fatal getaway attempt.

Curious spectators were beginning to assemble around the three corpses. A cowboy caught the two riderless horses and tied them to a rail in front of the Lucky Dollars Saloon.

"Will he live, doc?"

Sidlaw voiced the question with a curious passion in his tone as he turned to watch the doctor at work probing for the ambush bullet.

Frazer looked stern as he removed a sterilized probing instrument from a steaming pan.

"Hardly see how he can, stranger. Slug's lodged

in his vertebra, I'm afraid. But ol' Buck's made o' sawdust an' whang leather, an' I figger with luck maybe he'll hang on long enough to greet the Phantom Sheriff. Buck's lookin' for him any day now."

Spook grimaced as he saw the doctor swab the ugly wound. No doubt the high-velocity bullet had mushroomed after impact.

"The Phantom Sheriff?" queried Sidlaw. "Is that the same Phantom Sheriff I've heard tell of—the hombre who's been making a hobby o' tamin' wild towns over Texas way?"

"Yeah." The doctor's voice was musing. "The Mexicans named him the Phantom Sheriff because bullets seemed to dodge him. An' it's time he headed this way. Smoketree is wilder'n any town along the Rio Grande, I reckon."

"Buck Clawson sent for this Phantom Sheriff, did he?"

Joe Frazer gave the cowboy a puzzled glance, then picked up a scalpel.

"Guess you didn't know the Phantom Sheriff is ol' Buck's son, that he ain't seen since he was knee-high to the loadin' gate of a .30-30. His name is Freddie Clawson."

Pondering this news, Spook Sidlaw turned to leave, feeling that his presence in the doctor's office would only impede the medico.

He had to stop short at the doorway to keep from colliding with a girl who had ridden up outside. Flinging herself from her pinto, she had run into the doctor's office without pausing to tie up.

"I heard the shooting from up at the house and knew Dad must be in a jam," she cried. "Is . . . is he hurt bad, doc?"

Spook removed his gray Stetson as he saw the girl run to the sheriff's side and grip the unconscious man's gnarled old fist in her hands.

"Rustle me some bandages, Marie. In the top cabinet."

The cowboy from Wyoming watched the girl closely as the grief-stricken daughter of Buck Clawson hastened to obey the doctor's instructions.

Marie Clawson was the type of woman a Western man would want, Spook saw at his first quick appraisal. She was attractive in a lean, bronzed way, with tumbling clusters of sun-bleached hair under the sweeping brim of a cream Stetson, and the glow of ruddy, vibrant youth was under her wind-bitten skin.

Marie Clawson was bred to outdoor living and dressed accordingly in split-type doeskin skirt and an apricot-colored blouse. Sidlaw was conscious of a quick glance from eyes as blue as sage blossoms under a Wyoming sun.

"Who did it, doc?" Marie Clawson mastered the catch in her throat as she brought linen strips to Frazer. "You got any idea what happened?

Daddy was expecting trouble today. He was so moody at breakfast—"

Suddenly ill at ease, Spook trailed his spurs outside and went over to the throng which was engaged in hauling Les Padillo's corpse out of the water trough and stretching it beside Cameron's.

Prominent in the crowd was the frock-coated card sharp who had greeted Sidlaw from the porch of the Lucky Dollars Saloon on the waddy's inopportune arrival in Smoketree.

A moment later Sidlaw heard someone address the tall, black-mustached hombre as Gila Jack, and he knew that he was looking at the sinister gun boss of this wild border settlement.

Elbowing through the crowd, Spook Sidlaw squatted beside the carcass of his dead horse. Then, with a muffled oath, he began uncinching his Cheyenne stock saddle.

Helping hands lifted the inert bulk of the dead animal long enough for Sidlaw to extricate his kak, with its burden of soogan roll, saddlebags, and booted Winchester.

He carried the trail gear over to a sidewalk and laid it down. When he turned, it was to find Gila Jack Shadmer facing him through a curtain of bluish smoke that curled in twin jets from his nostrils.

"Too bad you lost your pony, son. I tried to warn you, remember? Right nice piece of horseflesh you were forking when you arrived in our fair city."

Sidlaw nodded, his eyes studying Gila Jack's swart, evil countenance. He found himself recoiling from the gaze of those buckshot eyes as if they had been the orbs of a snake.

"Yeah. Poor ol' crowbait! Won him last year in a poker game at Dodge. Top horse o' my string all winter."

"Aimin' to stop here, stranger?"

"Not any. I was headin' toward Alamogordo, honin' to rent my lass rope at some spread on the way. But it seems like ambush bullets are swarmin' round your town thicker'n buzzards at a hawg-killin', don't it?"

The crowd was quick to catch the suggestion in the tone of the man from Wyoming. Out of the corner of his eye Sidlaw noticed men edging away, as if apprehensive of trouble.

Gila Jack Shadmer grinned unpleasantly and flicked ash off his cigar with a manicured finger. Sidlaw had seen that fish-belly white on the tapering hands of card sharps many times before.

"Of course you didn't know what you were blunderin' into, stranger," Shadmer answered, a hint of menace behind his affability. "I tried to warn you you were stickin' your horns into the middle of a gun battle."

With studied deliberation the Wyoming drifter

fished in a pocket of his red-checkered shirt for a bag of tobacco and thin husks. With a deft manipulation of his right hand he rolled a quirly, tugged puckering string with his teeth, and stuck the brown-paper cigarette in his lips. At no time during the automatic smoke-building did his eyes leave the gambler's face.

"A right neat gun-fight it was, too—eh, Shadmer?" commented the waddy, thumbing flame from a match tip. "The sheriff nailed those two *ladrones* right slick for an oldster sufferin' with ague. Too bad he got drilled by an ambushin' snake, wasn't it?"

Gila Jack's brittle eyes regarded Sidlaw through a haze of cheroot smoke.

"Yeah. Too bad! I didn't see the shootin', myself. Figgered things was gittin' too hot to stay outdoors, so I ducked into my barroom."

Sidlaw's eyes ranged over the spectators, noting the subtle air of tension that had gripped the throng.

"You sure you didn't see that bushwackin', Shadmer?"

The gambler stiffened.

"That's what I said, cowboy. Any arguments?" The boss of the Lucky Dollars dive flicked back the tails of his coat to expose jewel-incrusted gun butts. "I might go so far as to ask you if *you* seen who fired the shot that downed Clawson, stranger."

Sidlaw hesitated. He read the signs plain enough. Shadmer was baiting him into a draw. And the visitor from up north had no way of proving the hunch that was slowly crystallizing in his brain. All he had to bank on was the whispered comment he had heard regarding Shadmer's hatred of the old sheriff.

"No argument," he parried. "Thar's no use me tarryin' here that I know of."

Sidlaw stooped to shoulder his belongings.

"Reckon I'll help myself to one o' them bandit's hosses that I roped an' brought back to town. One of 'em finished off my fuzztail, which was worth two o' theirs."

Shadmer followed the young waddy as Sidlaw made his way down to the hitch bar in front of the Lucky Dollars Saloon. Sidlaw sucked at his cigarette thoughtfully as he sized up the two nervous broncs that had been the late property of the outlaws whose corpses were now drawing flies over by the watering trough.

"Reckon I'll take this stove-up critter," decided Sidlaw, putting his hand on the mane of a bay mustang whose saddle bore the initials of Les Padillo. "Here's hopin' its owner was the one who killed my bronc. It'll sort o' balance things better."

Without further ado, Sidlaw stripped the outlaw's saddle from the bay and proceeded to cinch his own Wyoming hull aboard the mustang.

Shadmer, leaning against the saloon porch post, eyed the proceedings curiously.

"You're a bit hasty, stranger," suggested the gambler when Sidlaw commenced bridling Padillo's horse with his own split-ear headstall. "You ain't got any legal right to that horse. It'll be up to a judge to say whether you can claim ownership or not."

Spook Sidlaw strode up to the gambler and calmly flicked his half-smoked quirly to one side.

"What's it to you, Shadmer? Or was them bandits forkin' ponies out o' your private string, mebbe?"

It was a clear challenge, and one Shadmer could not pass up in public. With a quick oath the gun boss of Smoketree plummeted a white fist toward his revolver handle.

Crack! The impact of Sidlaw's knuckled fist against the gambler's jaw drowned the slap of Gila Jack's palm on his gun.

Eyes glazed by the terrific punch, the gambler fell back against the porch, then slumped to a sitting position, head wabbling on his shoulders, a thread of blood seeping from a battered chin.

"If I'd been more sure o' my ground, Shadmer, I'd 'a' bucked your play with gun smoke," declared the man from Wyoming as he casually mounted his new horse. "But your fight and Clawson's is no business of mine, so I reckon I'll shake the dust o' your mangy town offn my spurs right pronto."

After saying this, the cool-nerved stranger spurred at a canter down the street, his voice lifted in the clear, rollicking song he had been singing on his arrival.

CHAPTER IV.

Tangled thoughts roiled inside Spook Sidlaw's head as his new mount flung back the miles of Whispering Desert, putting the cow-town behind sandy, cactus-tufted ridges to the westward.

A slight sense of guilt, of leaving things unfinished back there in Smoketree, possessed the cowboy. Guilt that he had not remained in the tough border settlement to back Sheriff Clawson's play.

It was a nasty set-up, in Smoketree. Clearly, the town was dominated by the bullying gun boss, Gila Jack Shadmer. And with the sheriff probably slated for the cemetery before sundown, Shadmer would be in a position to turn Smoketree into a festering sinkhole of outlawry before the citizens of Malpais County could find another man with the guts to tackle Clawson's job.

Sidlaw thought of Marie Clawson, and his sense of discomfort increased.

"Reckon I let a perty girl's face booger me into wantin' to ram my horns where they ain't got any business," decided the rider. "Anyhow, the sheriff's kid is supposed to be on his way to help clean up that wolf nest. I only hope the Phantom Sheriff gets there before his father cashes in his chips."

Sidlaw gave his mount its head, slumped into a comfortable position in the saddle, and dozed. The heat of the summer day and accumulated trail fatigue dulled his senses.

Thus it was that the man did not spot the coiled diamondback rattler on the trail side until its sharp zzzzzz made the bay halt with a suddenness that threw Sidlaw's groin sharply against the swell-fork pommel.

Then, arching its back like a broken clock spring, Padillo's mustang commenced bucking.

Taken completely off guard, Sidlaw felt himself hurled overboard before he could seize horn or reins. But a tragic fate prevented him from merely being unhorsed.

His right boot, twisting in the tapaderoed oxbow stirrup, remained wedged in place. His head and shoulders slammed the sandy earth a bare two feet from the spot where the coiled rattlesnake buzzed its warning of poison death.

"Whoa, crow-bait!" Sidlaw gasped.

Padillo's horse was spooky with a new rider to begin with. Now, feeling a burden dragging from its stirrup, and panicked by the presence of the reptile under hoof, the mustang bolted.

Cactus and sandy hummocks blurred past under Sidlaw's sledding body as the horse shied off the trail and cut down a slope.

Head banging dizzily against the yielding sand, Sidlaw fought to extricate his boot from the clinging stirrup. With flailing arms he struggled to keep his body from being swept under the deadly, steel-shod rear hoofs of the galloping bay.

Then despair flooded Sidlaw as he saw the horse making for a rocky stretch of malpais bordering the foot of the sandy hill.

Once dragged into that acreage of sharp, flinty rock, his skull would be bashed open like an egg, if the horse's hammering hoofs did not beat his dragging body to pulped meat first. Whichever happened, violent death was certain.

Then Sidlaw's neck slapped hard against a protruding ignota root and his senses reeled. No longer did his arms claw into the ground to keep his body away from churning hoofs. He went lax as a straw-stuffed dummy.

New hoofbeats thundered into Sidlaw's dazed hearing. A shadow blotted out the sun alongside him. Dimly, he was aware of the fact that a horseman was speeding down the slope, crowding in between the rocky terrain and his own runaway bronc.

Leaning far from the saddle, the horseman seized the bit ring of Sidlaw's horse. Leaping from stirrups, the newcomer gouged spike-heeled boots into the rocks and gravel, bogging down the bronc's head.

Rubble showered. The runaway's muzzle was being forced groundward. Then, with a supreme effort, the cowboy out of nowhere bull-dogged his weight on the bridle and Spook Sidlaw felt the mad dash come to a dust-clouded halt.

"Steady, boy! Steady, theah!"

Sidlaw's throbbing ears picked up the stranger's words as the rider regained his feet and, still holding the blowing mustang by the bit, crossed in front of the horse and reached down to seize Sidlaw's ankle.

A jerk, and the twisted tapadero released him, allowing Sidlaw's aching leg to drop limply to the ground.

Rolling away from the horse, the dazed cowboy from Wyoming reached down to rub a throbbing hip as he saw his rescuer lead Padillo's mustang to a nearby pinon and hitch reins to bole.

Then the rider came back to where Spook Sidlaw lay groaning at the edge of the rock patch, his head reeling from the battering his brain had received during the dangerous slide down the hill.

"Reckon yore lucky stah ain't set yet, pardnah!" drawled his rescuer in a musical Texan brogue. He stooped to shoulder Sidlaw's hundred-and-seventy-pound bulk with apparent ease. "Ah'll get you in the shade an' then we'll see if yore laig is broke."

A few moments later, Spook Sidlaw was taking stock of his hurts in the shade of a paloverde. His red-checkered shirt had all but been ripped from his back, and his Stetson was lost somewhere back up the hillside.

Sand and brush had clawed hanks of hair from his scalp. The bones in his leg were uninjured, but muscles had been jerked cruelly and his knee and hip joints felt as if they were unsocketed.

"Reckon you saved my life that time, brother!" panted Spook Sidlaw gratefully. "If you hadn't been on the trail an' seen me get bucked off, I'd be in hell by now, I reckon."

Sidlaw tried to focus his vision on his rescuer. He saw a lanky rider of about his own age, with curly hair of a golden shade that reminded Sidlaw, oddly enough, of Marie Clawson's crisp ringlets.

"Ah see you have a canteen on yore saddle, suh," chuckled his rescuer. "Yuh'll feel better after yuh git some o' the grit washed out o' yore craw."

The young hombre returned with Sidlaw's canteen, and the waddy gulped eagerly of the tepid water, then poured a pint of it on his tousled head, letting the liquid seep into his scratched and bleeding scalp.

"Ah had to jump off my own pony," explained the blond stranger, "so if yuh ah all right, suh, ah'll borrow yore nag an' go rope him."

"You bet, pardner," answered Sidlaw, his voice shaky. "But don't trust him. Yuh see what he danged near done fer me."

Sidlaw propped himself against the trunk of the paloverde, grateful for the shade. His brain was still reeling from the effects of the accident, and it seemed that every sinew in his lean body was twisted and strained.

Spook saw his benefactor bowleg out to Padillo's mustang, unbuckle a coiled lariat and shake out a loop. Then, untying the skittery bronc, the waddy swung into the kak and spurred out onto the rock-carpeted malpais where his own horse was running loose, a hundred yards distant.

The riderless horse bolted at its master's approach, heading for the blue-gray hedge of smoketrees. Sidlaw admired the young Texan's bronc. It was a magnificent chestnut, leggy and deep-chested, with foam-flecked flanks thick with trail dust.

With deft horsemanship the stranger spurred Padillo's mustang toward the smoketrees where his own horse had vanished, lariat held out in casting position.

And then the desert air rocked to the crash of a triggered rifle.

With a scream of pain the young rider hurled both arms aloft, then clapped them hard to his side.

Spook Sidlaw reared to his feet, clinging to the paloverde branches as he stared off across the flat and saw his benefactor reeling in the saddle like a straw dummy.

Another shot echoed out of the chaparral to the west, and Spook Sidlaw, watching with face gray with horror, saw Padillo's horse collapse with the grim finality which bespoke a mortal wound.

Hurled free of the toppling horse, the wounded Texan staggered a few steps, seeking the shelter of the smoketrees.

Crack! For a third time the unseen rifleman hammered a slug at the lurching cowboy. The bullet kicked up a spat of sand and ricocheted into space.

Then a fourth shot exploded harshly on the sweltered air. This time the bullet again found its target, square in the cowboy's back. Knocked down by slamming lead, the youthful hombre flopped on his face and lay motionless in the sun.

Sidlaw wrenched himself out of his paralysis of horror and rage to claw at his own holsters, only to find them empty. His twin Peacemakers had evidently dropped from their holsters during his mad drag at a stirrup's end down the hillside.

Then hoofs rattled out in the chaparral from whence had come the ambush shots, and a burst of triumphant laughter reached Sidlaw's ears as he swayed against the paloverde. Staring off through the foliage, Spook Sidlaw saw the phantom shape of the mounted dry-gulcher spurring for the hogback ridge to regain the Smoketree trail.

"Gila Jack Shadmer!"

Sidlaw forced the words out of an aching throat as he recognized the frock-coated figure on the departing horse.

For a full ten seconds Sidlaw stared at the gambler as Shadmer loped over the skyline, bound for Smoketree.

"The dirty, murderin' devil!" Sidlaw muttered hoarsely. "He shot that young feller from ambush because he figgered he was shootin' *me!*"

Thunderstruck by the knowledge that the man who had saved his life had lost his own at the hands of a skulking killer who had actually been stalking someone else, Sidlaw started running across the rocks toward his fallen helper.

It was plain enough to figure out, this bush-whacking on Whispering Desert. Gila Jack Shadmer, his heart bitter with hatred because of the public beating he had received, had undoubtedly trailed Sidlaw out of Smoketree.

At two hundred yards' range, the gambler had taken for granted that the similarly dressed Texan riding Padillo's horse was Spook Sidlaw. Probably Shadmer had figured that Sidlaw was riding with lass rope unslung in pursuit of the Mexican bank robber's escaped horse.

Dropping to his knees alongside the bullet-riddled Texan, Sidlaw rolled the youth over on his back and looked down into a contorted, oyster-white face. To Spook's amazement, he was still breathing.

Death was beginning to glaze the young man's torture-bright eyes, and crimson foam bubbled from his lips as he tried to speak.

"Git word to my dad . . . about this . . . will yuh, amigo?" pleaded the dying waddy as Sidlaw cradled his golden-fleeced head on one elbow. "My dad . . . kin tally that skunk . . . foah me."

Spook swallowed hard and nodded.

"I'll tally him myself, kid!" he said softly. "What's yore dad's name, an' whar kin I find him?"

A death rattle was in the cowboy's throat as he struggled to keep the lids off his blue eyes.

"Dad's named . . . Buck Clawson," came the faint whisper. "He's sheriff . . . in the next town west o' heah. Ah'm . . . Freddie Clawson—"

Sidlaw felt his blood chill as he repeated the name, then stared harder at the dying youth in his arms.

This cowboy, who had saved him from certain death, was none other than the Rio Grande country's celebrated Phantom Sheriff!

CHAPTER V.

It seemed hard to believe that the Phantom Sheriff, whose name and deeds were familiar to men throughout the Western cattle country, could be this young, unwhiskered stripling.

Stories of the Phantom Sheriff's prowess had reached Spook Sidlaw many times during the years he had punched cattle up in Wyoming.

He had become a deputy sheriff, then a Texas Ranger, the story went. Superstitious Mexicans had given him his familiar nickname of the Phantom Sheriff because of his uncanny ability to escape their bullets. In fact, the sheriff's real name had never reached Sidlaw's ears that he could remember.

But Sidlaw did remember hearing that on his twentieth birthday the Phantom Sheriff had cleaned up a wild town on the Pecos with his own unorthodox but effective manner.

He had followed that victory by taming three more border towns, using a system that would have been barred him had his jurisdiction been restricted to a sheriff's county lines—six-gun methods which had put the fear of death into owl-hoot riders whenever they heard that the Phantom Sheriff was riding their territory.

And now Freddie Clawson had been riding

west to rejoin his father, game old Buck Clawson of Malpais County, Arizona.

But Fate, in the form of Gila Jack Shadmer, had written finish to the Phantom Sheriff's career. Here, within five miles of Smoketree, where Freddie's father likewise lay in the shadow of eternity, probably a victim of the same Winchester .30-30 that had put the stamp of doom on the Phantom Sheriff.

"Listen, Freddie!" whispered Spook Sidlaw, his lips close to the dying waddy's ear. "Kin yuh hear me? I jest come from Smoketree. In fact, I jest left yore sister, Marie, an' yore father. They . . . they're both fine an' dandy, Freddie, an' are expectin' yuh. Yuh got to live fer them."

Freddie Clawson opened his eyes and Sidlaw saw the spark of life brighten somewhat at his words.

"Marie? Yuh see Sis?" The Phantom Sheriff's ash-gray lips bent in a smile in spite of his agony. "Marie's a beaut, ain't she? She'll be nineteen tomorrow, Marie will. That was one reason Ah been larrupin' my cayuse so hahd, this past week. Ah wanted to reach Smoketree in time to celebrate Marie's birthday with dad."

A shudder passed through the Phantom Sheriff's frame.

"Ah'm playin' . . . out . . . my string . . . fast, amigo!" whispered Freddie Clawson. "Befoah Ah go . . . take gold badge . . . out of chaps

45

pocket. Give it . . . to Marie. *Sabe usted*? Ah don't want her to fo'git her brothah. She was only a tike o' nine when Ah saw her last—"

Clawson panted heavily as Spook Sidlaw unbuttoned a pocket of his bat-wing chaps and withdrew therefrom a six-pointed star made of solid gold, which glittered blindingly in the sun rays.

"I shore will, Freddie!" promised the Wyoming buckaroo. "An' I'll do more'n that. I know the polecat who ambushed you. Feller name of Gila Jack Shadmer. I won't rest until Shadmer's name is carved on a boothill stone, Freddie. You saved my life this afternoon, took a slug meant fer my gizzard. So I'm promisin' yuh I'll avenge this—"

Bitterness clouded the Phantom Sheriff's eyes, which were rapidly losing their luster before the approach of death.

"Shadmah . . . got me, huh? Dad writ me about Shadmah. Heah's hopin' . . . you do wing that gun hawk, suh. He was the hombre . . . Ah was ridin' west . . . to extuhminate foah dad."

Spook Sidlaw bent lower as Freddie's voice trailed off.

"Cowboy . . . Ah want Marie . . . to have that gold badge. An' take my hoss . . . to dad. Tell 'em Ah—"

Sidlaw straightened, winking his own misty lashes hard as he realized the significance of young Clawson's slumping muscles.

46

"Adios, kid!" breathed Sidlaw as he gently lowered the Phantom Sheriff's lifeless body to the ground. "I reckon I'll take up yore battle whar you left off, Freddie. I'll clean up the job o' town-tamin' you was comin' west to finish fer yore dad!"

Sidlaw stared at the golden star in his palm. It was no ordinary lawman's badge. Engraved on the furbished emblem were three words which gave its bearer jurisdiction beyond the boundaries reared by politicians. Authority perhaps not recognized by legal statute books, but respected and feared on the out trails where lead was law.

The three words were: THE PHANTOM SHERIFF.

Turning the amazing star over in his palm, Sidlaw read small words carved into the gold on the reverse side next to the pin:

> Badge presented to Freddie Clawson in grateful appreciation of what he did to make Del Moro, Texas, a decent town to live in. *Buena fortuna*!
>   Citizen's Committee

Slowly, Spook Sidlaw got to his feet. No longer was he a carefree drifter, roaming over the West with no responsibilities other than obtaining food and shelter for himself and mount.

A six-gun destiny had placed a sacred trust in his keeping—a mission that could be written off as "paid" only by gun smoke and guts. Not only was it a responsibility he owed Freddie Clawson, the game young lawman who had lost his life assisting Spook Sidlaw. It was something far deeper and more significant than that now.

Spook Sidlaw's fate had been interwoven with the unfinished drama which Sheriff Buck Clawson had waged in the wild border town of Smoketree.

That same destiny which had caused Sidlaw to witness what was probably the final chapter to Sheriff Clawson's career as a Western peace officer was now sending Sidlaw back to Smoketree, carrying the Phantom Sheriff's golden badge of office.

A few yards away, Padillo's mustang was cropping grama grass among the rocks. The bronc made no effort to bolt as Spook mounted him—a task made difficult by his aching bones and muscles.

Beyond the rocky patch, at the fringe of the smoketree chaparral, young Clawson's chestnut was nibbling grass, its reins tangled in a dwarf mesquite.

Five minutes later, Sidlaw was tying Freddie Clawson's corpse to his own saddle for the trek back to Smoketree. Then, trailing the chestnut at rope's end, the Wyoming puncher headed back along the hillside. He dismounted three times en route to recover his fallen six-guns and his Stetson.

The sun was sinking behind the craggy spine of the Dragoon Mountain range when Sidlaw's slow-pacing horses once more emerged from the cactus thickets of Whispering Desert.

Approaching the main street from the north, Spook halted in the rear of Dr. Frazer's home, remembering that the old medico also held the official title of Malpais County's coroner. He found Frazer cooking supper in his kitchen and broke the news of Freddie's death to him as Frazer came out to inspect the body.

"This'll finish off the sheriff!" Frazer groaned as Sidlaw helped carry the body into a room which served as morgue. "The old man wanted to die in his own house. He ain't got a chance. So I took him to his home up on Mescal Hill about three hours ago. Marie's up thar with him now, pore kid."

Frazer invited Sidlaw to join him at supper, and the trail-weary puncher gladly accepted. He found himself drawn to the apple-cheeked old cow-town doctor, whose blue eyes twinkled with benevolence.

"How come Freddie Clawson wasn't livin' with his father an' sister?" Sidlaw asked after they had finished eating.

"Seems they was livin' back in the Texas

49

Panhandle," explained Frazer, lighting up a corncob. "Mrs. Clawson got T.B. an' Buck brought her out hyar to Smoketree. He left Freddie back in Texas to finish school, while Marie—she was only nine year old then—come out here to be with her mother. In the meantime Freddie became the Phantom Sheriff, carved out a name fer hisself on his own hook. This was to have been their first reunion in ten years."

Sidlaw shook his head grimly.

"I really wish I could 'a' took them slugs Gila Jack Shadmer meant fer me, doc," he said sincerely, rising from the table. "Well, now comes the hard part of it. I got to go up an' break the news to Marie Clawson—an' give her her brother's gold star, here."

He left his saddlebags and other gear with Frazer, stabled the mustang in the coroner's private barn at the rear of the lot, and then set off toward Mescal Hill, leading Freddie Clawson's horse behind him.

He dreaded the task that faced him, the job of bearing the grim tidings of Freddie's murder to Marie Clawson. He found himself almost hoping that the sheriff had died, so that the old man would be spared the final crushing news of his boy's death.

He would far rather have sought out Gila Jack Shadmer in the latter's den at the Lucky Dollars Saloon to pay the Phantom Sheriff's murder debt in gun smoke. But that could wait. He had to carry out Freddie's instructions about his gold badge and horse before he did anything else.

A light twinkled in the cottage that had been the Clawson home during the past years, as Sidlaw tied the chestnut to the front gate.

Then, removing his sombrero, he walked up the gravel path toward the house, steeling himself for the ordeal that faced him.

At the same moment, down in Gila Jack Shadmer's saloon, the gambler was listening to startling information from a Mexican swamper, jabbering in Spanish:

"I saw him coming out of Senor Frazer's just now, yes! They were talking about a dead man. Senor Shadmer, with my own eyes I saw it! This hombre you rode out of town to kill—he is even now walking up Mescal Hill toward Senor Clawson's *casa*!"

Shadmer got up from his desk, hitching his gun belts ominously.

"I must have shot the wrong man out in Whispering Desert this afternoon then," he mused. "Reckon I'll take a *pasear* up to Buck's house an' settle that Wyomin' buckaroo's hash fer once an' all. Fer all I know, mebbe he saw me shoot that stranger—an' brung the carcass back to town. Anyhow, I better play things safe an' git that salty buckaroo out o' the way."

CHAPTER VI.

Marie Clawson opened the door to Spook Sidlaw's knock. In the lamp glow he could see the girl struggling hard to keep back her emotions.

"You are the man who helped my father after the shooting," she said in a dull, tired voice. "I . . . I want to thank you for that, and for coming here now to see how he is. But I'd rather be alone—now—"

Sidlaw fingered his sombrero brim awkwardly.

"I kin understand that, miss. But if you'd—"

"Dr. Frazer is coming in a few minutes with some ladies to help me," the sheriff's daughter whispered chokingly. "Now—I must get back to dad—"

"I got—somethin' to give you, miss. From yore brother."

Marie Clawson paused in the act of shutting the door, her brows arching with interest.

"From Freddie? Is he in town? Why doesn't he come here? That's all that dad's hanging on for—to see Freddie once again!"

Mutely, Spook Sidlaw handed the girl the solid-gold star engraved, "The Phantom Sheriff." She stared at it several seconds before its significance filtered into her brain.

Then she looked up, her larkspur-blue eyes glowing.

"You . . . you are my brother?"

Sidlaw swallowed hard, wishing he could be anywhere else but where he was. He debated mentally whether to let the news of her brother's death go until later.

Marie was quick to note his confusion and gripped his wrist with a strong, icy hand.

"Tell me—Freddie gave you this badge? Did something—happen to my brother?"

Sidlaw took a deep breath and then blurted out the facts. He told her his name, repeated Freddie Clawson's dying words to the best of his memory.

Admiration for Marie Clawson's courage welled through Spook's veins as he saw her take the blow without flinching, then slowly steel herself against the reaction she knew would come.

"I promised Freddie just afore he—went," continued Sidlaw, "that I'd carry on for him until Gila Jack's been gun-blasted out o' Smoketree, miss. An' I guess thar's no time like the present to start in. I might as well have a showdown with Shadmer tonight, I reckon."

Marie blanched as she saw Sidlaw's hands drop to the white bone handles of his belted six-guns. Then, with an impulsive gesture, she pressed the gold badge of the Phantom Sheriff into his palm.

"Listen, Mr. Sidlaw!" she cried. "Daddy's in the bedroom there. He's barely conscious and I know he can't see anything. He keeps asking for Freddie. I wonder—would you—pin on this badge—and pretend like you're my brother? So daddy can go—happy—thinking that—"

Tenderly, Spook patted the girl's arm, and looked away while Marie dabbed her eyes with the corner of a neckerchief.

"Shore. We kin git away with it *bueno*, Miss Marie. Yore dad ain't seen Freddie since he was a button."

With an impulsive movement, Marie Clawson pinned the gold badge of the Phantom Sheriff to his torn shirt. Then, taking his rope-calloused hand in her own, the girl led the way into a dimly lighted bedroom off the parlor.

Sheriff Buck Clawson lay on a white-sheeted bed, his face haggard with pain, talonlike fingers plucking the quilt's hem. His eyes were closed and his breath came in laboring gasps.

"Daddy!" Marie's voice was vibrant as the two knelt alongside the old sheriff's bed. She reached for the knob which controlled the wick of the bedside lamp, turning down the flame until a mere glow suffused Spook Sidlaw's bronzed face. "Daddy—I have wonderful news. Freddie just rode into town!"

New life seemed to surge through the wounded sheriff as he turned his head and directed half-closed eyes upon the cowboy who reached out a hand to grasp the lawman's.

"Howdy—dad!" husked Sidlaw, trying to put assurance into his voice. "Didn't I tell yuh I'd git hyar fer Marie's birthday tomorrow? Waal, hyar I am!"

Tears coursed down the sheriff's cheeks as he ran his other hand up Spook's sleeve, where he groped for and felt the glittering gold star that was only an unfocused blur in his own eyes.

"Freddie . . . I knowed yuh'd git here afore I cashed in, son," breathed the dying oldster. "I cain't see yore face very well, son. But I kin see yuh've filled out into a husky specimen. Yuh'll find lots o' work . . . fer that Phantom Sheriff's badge . . . hyar in Smoketree, Freddie. I'm afeared I won't be here . . . to back yore play."

"Yuh'll be fit as a fiddle in a few days, dad!" retorted the cowboy. "It takes more'n a chunk o' lead to salt down a Clawson; you know that."

Buck smiled feebly.

"A chip offn the old block, Freddie," whispered the sheriff of Malpais County. "Take good keer . . . o' Marie . . . won't yuh, son?"

"I shore will, dad." Spook Sidlaw gulped hard, his brain racing. He could not risk too much talk for fear of ruining their merciful deception.

"I jest . . . been waitin' . . . fer yuh, Freddie," sighed Buck Clawson. "Good luck, boy. Watch Shadmer . . . like yuh would . . . a snake. An'

55

keep an eye . . . on Marie. She's growed up . . . into a fine woman. She—"

Marie buried her head against Spook's shoulder as they saw Buck Clawson's hand fall away from the Phantom Sheriff badge on Sidlaw's shirt front.

The waddy's eyes glinted with horror and grief as he saw death relax Buck Clawson's features—a face wreathed in a smile of happiness as he carried into eternity the belief that he had been reunited with his only son in his last few moments on earth.

Spook stood up, gently taking Marie's hands in his.

"Buck up, miss. Yore dad went—happy—thinkin' his family was with him at the end. I'm glad—about that—anyhow."

Sensing the girl's desire to be alone with her father for a moment or two, Spook tiptoed out into the front room. She followed him shortly, and as he met her eyes he felt a strange inner surging in his heart.

"Mr. Sidlaw—you said you were going to carry on—for Freddie?"

He nodded, shifting his feet awkwardly.

"Reckon I am, miss. Yuh see, I owe my life to him. I wasn't worth a fine young feller like yore brother losin' his life on my account. The least I kin do—is square things with Shadmer."

She came to stand before him.

"I've only known you ten minutes—Spook," she said softly. "But already I owe you much, for giving my dad the greatest happiness he has known since mother died, six years ago. I'll never forget that."

Sidlaw fumbled at the Phantom Sheriff's badge on his shirt.

"Reckon yuh'll treasure this star, miss," he said. "Yore brother's dyin' request was that I give it to yuh. You kin be proud of it till yore dyin' day, Miss Marie, an' fer what it stands for—"

She caught his hand as he began unpinning the gold emblem.

"Would you—give that badge back to me—when you've finished Freddie's job for him, Spook? Somehow—I think Freddie would like it that way. I know Daddy would, if he knew. And I know what a vow means to a man, out here in the West. I know you won't stop—until you've fulfilled your pledge to Freddie. Maybe it'll bring you luck—to become the Phantom Sheriff in his place."

Sidlaw, his eyes meeting the girl's blue gaze, understood.

"*Gracias*, miss. I'll be honored to wear it. An' when I've finished the job Freddie come out to Arizona to do, I'll return this star to yuh."

Footsteps grated on the gravel path outside, and the girl rubbed her eyes and tried to compose herself.

"That will be Dr. Frazer coming back, Spook," she said. "He'll—take care of things."

Spook shook hands awkwardly, then stepped to the door, anxious to greet Frazer first and spare Marie Clawson the pain of having to announce her father's death to the doctor.

Stepping out into the cool desert night, he saw a sombreroed man waiting at the step.

"Buck just passed on, doc," whispered Spook Sidlaw. "Marie's takin' it like a thoroughbred. But I'm glad you've come—"

Crash! Without warning, the man Sidlaw assumed to be Dr. Frazer lashed up an arm that held a steel-muzzled Colt .45. The barrel dented through Spook's jaw to scrape bone.

Caught off guard, Spook Sidlaw fell sideways off the doorstep to roll out on the lawn. A thousand stars rained across his vision as he recognized Gila Jack Shadmer's towering form straddling his prone body.

"Reckon it's adios fer you, busky!" came the gambler's throaty snarl. "I'm blowin' yore brains out right here an' now!"

So saying, the gun boss of Smoketree thumbed his six-gun to full cock and pressed the cold bore between Spook Sidlaw's eyes.

CHAPTER VII.

Paralysis seemed to freeze Spook Sidlaw's muscles as he struggled to reach his own guns.

The pressure of Shadmer's Colt muzzle on the bridge of his nose was like the cold touch of doom. A split second and the gun boss of Smoketree would trigger a slug through his skull, spatter his brains out on the lawn.

Then a blinding swath of lamplight fell over the scene, momentarily halting Shadmer's trigger finger.

Jerking his head about, Gila Jack Shadmer was in time to see that Marie Clawson had thrown the front door open and was staring at him, wide-eyed with horror.

Then, with a scream of anger, Marie Clawson hurled herself at the crouched killer as he straddled the prostrate form of the man from Wyoming.

Thrown off balance by the girl's unexpected attack, Shadmer chewed out an angry oath as he tried to fling Marie's hammering fists aside, then felt her seize his gun arm with both hands.

The moment's respite gave Spook Sidlaw opportunity to unkink his throbbing muscles. Rearing to his feet, the dazed waddy clawed six-guns from holsters.

With a savage blow, Shadmer hurled the girl aside, throwing her against the house wall.

Sidlaw's right-hand Colt bellowed its death song, but even at the pointblank range the half-stunned waddy saw that he had missed his target.

Gila Jack Shadmer fell back a step as he felt Sidlaw's bullet clip fabric from the collar of his gambler's coat.

With a yell, Spook Sidlaw charged the gun boss of Smoketree. Then hoofbeats thundered to a halt at the front gate, followed by excited voices.

A man was dismounting, running forward. Behind him, two other riders were leaving their horses, heading for the house.

Gila Jack Shadmer cursed fiercely as he leaped out of the bar of light cast by the open door, even as Spook Sidlaw fired again, his hands shaking as if from ague.

Rage consumed Shadmer as he vanished in the darkness, heading for the black hedge which bordered the lawn. There were too many odds to buck now, what with three newcomers arriving to back Sidlaw's play.

"What's up?" yelled the foremost of the oncoming trio.

It was Doc Frazer's voice, and Gila Jack Shadmer suspected that the two figures following the coroner in the darkness were Sammy Duncan and Dick Cordell, deputy sheriffs under Buck Clawson.

"It's Gila Jack!" came a cry from Marie Clawson, who was picking herself up over by the doorway. "He followed Mr. Sidlaw up here and jumped him when he opened the door."

"Yeah," came Sidlaw's groaning voice as he teetered on his feet, still dizzy with pain. "An' if Marie hyar hadn't bucked him, I'd be deader'n a tick in sheep-dip by now!"

Crash! Shadmer triggered three fast shots at the darkness which shrouded the Wyoming buckaroo.

Splinters showered the back of Sidlaw's neck as the wildly aimed slugs bit into the house clapboards. He eared back the knurled hammers of his Colts and sprayed the dark line of the hedge with slugs, firing at the spot where he had seen Gila Jack's gun flash.

But the escaping gambler had not paused in the spot where he had flung his shots at his invisible enemy.

Racing at top speed along the hedge, his fleeing form made invisible against the backdrop of darkness because of his bannering frock coat and blue Levi's, Shadmer hurdled a low picket fence and raced toward the horses at the front gate.

Sparks flew as steel-shod hoofs pounded gravel. Even as Spook Sidlaw raced past Doc Frazer and the other two arrivals on the gravel walk, he saw the blurred form of the escaping outlaw disappearing in the gloom down the hillside.

"Stole one o' yore hosses to make his gitaway, doc," panted Sidlaw, holstering his six-guns and turning to face the coroner. "But we got enough on Shadmer to hang the skunk. Thar warn't no mistakin' his identity when he gun-whipped me thar by the door."

Then, for the first time, Sidlaw saw that the two people who had accompanied Doc Frazer to the Clawson home were women.

"Meet Mrs. Venable an' Mrs. Beechey," said the coroner. "I brung 'em up to stay with Marie tonight."

The two housewives acknowledged Sidlaw's nod and then hurried over to where Marie Clawson stood by the doorway. After the three women had gone back inside, Frazer said:

"How's Buck?"

Sidlaw's grim headshake was his answer.

The two men stood side by side in the darkness, listening to the sound of Shadmer's escaping horse as the hoofbeats died behind the buildings on the outskirts of Smoketree, which lay in a sprawl of twinkling yellow lights at the foot of Mescal Hill.

"Reckon I won't be of any use around hyar now, doc," spoke the cowboy finally. "I'm goin' to trail Shadmer pronto, for fear he'll skip town when he realizes you was a witness to him shootin' at me jest now. He'll know we got too much on him fer it to be safe fer him to stick around Smoketree."

Frazer put a restraining hand on the cowboy's wrist.

"It'd be plumb suicide to buck Shadmer at his saloon tonight, Spook," warned the old medico gruffly. "He's got a gang o' paid gunnies in his barroom who'd be waitin' to rub yuh out."

"I cain't risk him gittin' away tonight, doc."

"I don't think," said Frazer in an odd tone, "that Gila Jack will hightail it, like you think. You don't realize the grip Shadmer's got on this town, son. An' now that Buck's gone—he'll be pizener'n ever."

Sidlaw's brows arched in surprise.

"You don't realize," Frazer went on, "that all three o' Buck Clawson's depities turned in their badges tonight when I told 'em Buck was due to pass in his chips. Thar ain't a depity in Smoketree who'd dare step into Buck's shoes an' buck Shadmer."

The cowboy gritted his jaws in disgust.

"What kind o' yaller-striped men does Arizona breed, anyhow, that they'd let a tinhorn gambler ramrod a town thisaway?"

The coroner flushed and spoke grimly.

"Gila Jack Shadmer is more'n a tinhorn gambler, son. He owns the big Lazy Diamond outfit over in the Dragoon foothills—over a hundred sections o' Malpais County's best grazin' kentry. That makes him range hog o' Malpais County, without a rancher in these parts who'd dare buck him an' his gun-packin' rustler outfit."

Sidlaw scowled. A saloon owner in the rustling business!

"If Shadmer's such a *malo hombre*, how come Uncle Sam ain't sent a Federal marshal down hyar to help out the sheriff?"

"The gov'ment's lost three marshals already, investigatin' rumors that Gila Jack is linked up with Francisco Yuma's big smugglin' gang that operates out o' Old Mexico. But the Federal people ain't ever been able to prove anything on Shadmer. He's as slippery as a greased eel an' dangerous as a rattler in dog days, Spook. Lightnin' with his guns, an' afraid o' nothin'."

Sidlaw stared into the night, his mind busy as they strolled out toward the gate.

He was beginning to realize that wiping out Shadmer and taming Smoketree was no mere matter of a gun-fight with a gambler. Apparently Shadmer's criminal operations were far-reaching indeed if they included wholesale cattle thievery and border hopping.

"I might 'a' known Shadmer was a big gun, else the sheriff wouldn't 'a' sent fer his son to clean up Smoketree," admitted Sidlaw as they reached the front fence. "But a good start will be fer me to put Shadmer in boothill tonight. I got a personal excuse to go gunnin' fer him now, yuh know."

The two men inspected the three horses at the gate. Not until then did Sidlaw realize that Shadmer had stolen Freddie Clawson's leggy chestnut in making his getaway.

"That's another score agin' Shadmer," cried Sidlaw angrily. "Freddie wanted his sister to have that chestnut. But bein' afoot won't keep me from badgerin' Shadmer in his saloon. Yuh see, doc, Marie sort o' made me the . . . the new Phantom Sheriff."

Doc Frazer eyed the cowboy's shirt, hanging in tatters from his bruised shoulders as a result of his narrow escape from death that afternoon when his boot had wedged in the stirrup.

"Better put on my coat, son," advised the medico, unbuckling a slicker from behind his saddle cantle and handing it to the waddy. "This cold night air won't help yuh much, the way yuh're stove up. If yuh're honin' fer a showdown with Gila Jack, yuh'll need to move as fast as possible. A warm coat'll help unkink them stiff muscles o' yourn."

Realizing the truth of the doctor's words, Spook Sidlaw donned the coat, grateful for its protection against the chill wind that was rapidly numbing his bruised torso.

"Thanks, doc. An' wish me luck. Bein' the Phantom Sheriff ain't the easiest job to hold up. *Hasta la vista.*"

Doc Frazer lifted an arm in farewell, let it drop.

"Adios, feller. I'm bettin' you do the job as well as the real Phantom Sheriff would 'a' done."

A strange thrill coursed through Sidlaw's being as he strode down the steep hillside toward the twinkling lights of town. He was, in truth, the Phantom Sheriff—carrying on for the daring young Texicano whose feats of daring had earned him that nickname, as well as the gold badge which Sidlaw now wore.

As Sidlaw neared the adobe-walled *jacal* huts of the Mexican quarter, his slitted eyes beheld a dark figure approaching on horseback up the trail. By the rider's sugar-loaf sombrero and bannering serape, Sidlaw recognized the oncomer as a Mexican peon.

"Senor Shadmer? I have the message for you, *si*."

Sidlaw stiffened and came to a halt as the peon's sibilant whisper greeted him from the darkness. The Mexican leaned from the saddle and thrust a piece of paper into Sidlaw's hand.

"I tried to find you at the Lucky Dollars Cantina when I rode into Smoketree tonight, senor," the peon continued in Spanish. "They told me you would be walking on this trail, *si*."

Sidlaw grasped enough Mexican to understand the peon's words, and was on the verge of turning the paper back to the mounted peon when the Mexican's slurred voice mentioned a name that brought a tingle of apprehension to the nape of his neck.

"Francisco Yuma is waiting at Cartridge Peak, Senor Shadmer. We will see you later, no?"

Before Sidlaw could answer, the Mexican had wheeled his horse and had ridden off into the darkness in the direction of the border.

"Francisco Yuma!" panted Sidlaw, making his way into a side street. "That's the name o' the big smugglin' king that Shadmer's supposed to be dealin' with!"

Excitement coursing through his veins, the new Phantom Sheriff made his way to the rear of Doc Frazer's house and admitted himself through the rear door.

Shutting the door carefully behind him, he scratched a match and lighted a lamp on the table where he and Frazer had eaten supper.

Then he unfolded the grimy piece of paper which the mysterious Mexican horseman said had come from the smuggling chief of the border country, Francisco Yuma.

"Reckon as how I'm the Phantom Sheriff now, I'll make it my business to read Shadmer's mail, especially letters that links him up with smugglers!" Sidlaw muttered to himself. "I wonder—"

His voice trailed off into an aghast whisper as he read the scribbled message intended for the gun boss of Smoketree—a missive which an amazing destiny had placed in his hands tonight because the doctor's slicker had resembled Shadmer's frock coat:

SENOR SHADMER:

My trusted *mozo*, Pancho Pedro, brings this to you, to inform you of tonight's password. Because several new opium buyers will meet with us on Cartridge Peak tonight, it will be necessary for each member to give the password to the sentinel in order to identify himself as one of us.

The password will be "Santa Sabatino" and the meeting place will be the same as last month. See you at midnight.

FRANCISCO YUMA.

CHAPTER VIII.

The Phantom Sheriff crumpled the smuggler chief's message in a damp fist. A confusion of thoughts ran riot in his head as he pondered this angle of the character of Gila Jack Shadmer.

From his conversation with the coroner, Sidlaw deduced that one of Buck Clawson's ambitions had been to smash the smuggling gang which was running contraband across the border near Smoketree.

"Because I was wearin' doc's slicker tonight, that Mexie figgered I was Shadmer wearin' that gambler's coat," muttered the cowboy softly. "Now I'm in a position to play Gila Jack Shadmer's part at this secret meetin' o' border hoppers at midnight. I wonder whar this Cartridge Peak is?"

Shucking the doctor's coat, Sidlaw stripped off the frayed remnants of his red-checkered shirt and then proceeded to unbuckle his own saddlebags which he had left in Frazer's kitchen. He donned a fresh shirt, then proceeded to inspect his twin .45s.

That done, Sidlaw left the coroner's home by the back door and walked out on the main street.

Carousing waddies drifted along the sidewalks, singing ribald songs as they made their tour of the gambling joints and saloons which lined Smoketree's main stem. But Spook Sidlaw directed his steps toward the yellow-lighted windows of Gila Jack Shadmer's establishment.

So large was the Lucky Dollars Saloon, with its dance-hall annex and adjoining gambling hall, that it flanked the main street for better than half a block. Its imposing size and the customers it attracted were testimony to the power and wealth of the town's outlaw boss.

Instead of entering the barroom through any of its three doorways, Sidlaw made a circuit of the building. His eyes probed the starlit gloom in hopes of seeing Freddie Clawson's stolen bronc somewhere, thereby indicating that Shadmer had returned to his saloon after his dash from Sheriff Clawson's home.

But Sidlaw found no trace of young Clawson's chestnut saddler. A private stable and corral occupied the rear half of Shadmer's block, but the Phantom Sheriff realized the folly of snooping around Shadmer's private property in the dark.

Making his way back to the front of the saloon, the Phantom Sheriff shouldered through the batwing doors into the tobacco-clouded barroom.

Gambling tables were ringed by whiskered hombres bucking the tiger at poker, roulette, and craps. Drinkers bellied the long mahogany bar from end to end.

Accosting a shaggy-headed bartender with the

70

name "Curly Bardoo" stenciled on his grimy apron, Sidlaw asked a question:

"I'm honin' to speak with Gila Jack. He in his office?"

Curly Bardoo sized up the sheriff swiftly. He wiped his hands on a bar rag, went to a side door, and looked into a darkened room. Then he turned and shook his head.

"Shadmer ain't in. Ain't been here fer an hour. But he'll be showin' up around nine o'clock, when the faro game opens. Anything I kin do fer yuh, stranger?"

The Phantom Sheriff thanked Bardoo and trailed his spurs back outdoors. There was nothing to be gained by hanging around the Lucky Dollars barroom, where he might possibly be recognized by one of Shadmer's paid gunmen. As it was, he was pretty sure that his brief visit inside Shadmer's place had passed without anyone giving him undue attention.

Down the street was a squat building with a tarpaper roof. Weather-peeled paint on the false front labeled the shack as "All-American Restaurant. Willie Wong, Prop."

"Good place to git information, I reckon," mused the waddy as he noted that the place was empty except for a moon-faced Chinaman.

"Kin you tell me whar Cartridge Peak is—how far it is from Smoketree, pardner?"

Sidlaw put the question as Willie Wong pattered

up to the front of the store in answer to the soft tinkle of a brass bell connected to the screen door.

Smiling with the bland geniality of his race, the yellow-skinned Chinese led Sidlaw to the front porch and pointed off through the night to where a pyramid-shaped mountain loomed on the southwestern horizon, some ten miles away.

"That be Ca'tlidge Peak, cowboy. She six, mebbe eight mile off, I leckon so."

Sidlaw thanked the Chinaman and headed across the street toward the coroner's home. Going to Frazer's stable, he saddled up Les Padillo's mustang, pleased to find that the bronc's temper had been quieted by his recent rubdown and graining.

No one saw the Phantom Sheriff as the newcomer from Wyoming cantered out of town by a back street which snaked through the dingy, vile-smelling Mexican quarter. He headed off across Whispering Desert in the direction of the rugged volcanic pile which Willie Wong had told him was Cartridge Peak.

Low, scudding cloud masses darkened the heavens, but Sidlaw's wide-pupiled eyes had no difficulty in keeping the towering bulk of Cartridge Peak before him, the rocky landmark serving as a guide.

The mustang which had belonged to the ill-fated bank robber proved to be a powerful one, with plenty of bottom and the uncanny sense which desert-bred horses acquire of picking out a trail through the mesquites and tornillo brush.

A half-hour after his departure from Smoketree, the going got rougher as Sidlaw reached the long, sweeping foothill which terminated in the craggy summit of Cartridge Peak.

Forced to slow to a walk because of the flinty soil under hoof, the mustang worked up the slope until the heavier chaparral gave way to the sparse vegetation of the upper altitudes.

Dimly, through what starlight managed to penetrate the overcast sky, Sidlaw made out a cairn of rock which government surveyors had erected to mark the international boundary line.

The bleak malpais of the Mexican province of Sonora stretched off to the southward, sinister and forbidding, abode of owl-hooters who sought the refuge of soil beyond the jurisdiction of American sheriffs or marshals.

From off in the distance somewhere the Phantom Sheriff could hear the murmur of water sluicing down a rock-ribbed canyon. That, according to what brief study Sidlaw had made of border maps, would be the Rio Piedras, which sprang from a fountainhead on Cartridge Peak.

"If I'm goin' to set in on Francisco Yuma's smuggler meetin' tonight I wish I knowed fer shore whar their meetin' place is," grunted the waddy from Wyoming. "Pancho Pedro's note didn't say whar, so it seems that Shadmer's been in a habit o' contactin' this smugglin' outfit, like Buck Clawson figgered."

As the mustang worked its way slowly out of a dry wash, Sidlaw took advantage of the dark rock walls about him to thumb a match from the snakeskin band of his Stetson, light it and consult his pocket watch.

"Eleven-forty," he grunted, blowing out the match and roweling the mustang lightly. "Francisco Yuma said he'd expect Shadmer by midnight. I reckon the other smugglers are up thar ahead of me somewhar."

He made his way out of the coulee, every nerve and fiber of his being atingle with suspense. Playing the role of Gila Jack Shadmer, with little more than a secret password to gain his entry to the outlaw council, might very well end with death.

But he had drawn cards in tonight's perilous game, and he intended to play them to his last white chip. The element of darkness was in his favor, for it would mask his face.

The mustang flung up its hammer-head and snorted warily as they pushed on up the desolate slope. Spook Sidlaw, head cocked and eardrums straining, could see or hear no sign of danger. Yet the horse was uneasy over something beyond the veil of the cloudy night.

"*Manos altos*, hombre! Stop!"

Out of a shadow-blotted nest of talus boulders dead ahead came a snakelike hiss.

With pulses racing, the Phantom Sheriff drew rein. He lifted his arms above his head as he dimly made out a sombreroed form emerging from the rocks, faint starlight glinting off the leveled barrel of a Winchester carbine.

"Who ees eet, *por favor?*" came the husky voice of his challenger. "You are covered, senor. Who ees eet?"

Sidlaw, muffling his voice to make it sound as near like Shadmer's nasal tone as possible, answered:

"Ain't you ever heard o' Gila Jack, amigo? I'm reportin' from Smoketree."

The sentry halted a few feet away, rifle still leveled at the cowboy's heart.

"Then *porque* you no geev the password, Senor Shadmer? Pancho Pedro said he gave eet to you een Smoketree tonight."

The waddy stiffened with dread as he caught the open suspicion in the sentry's words. He forced himself to give a low, careless chuckle.

"Shore I saw Pancho Pedro. The password, amigo, is Santa Sabatino."

The rifle lowered, and the Mexican stepped aside.

" *'Sta bueno.* You weel find Senor Yuma and the others camped on the reemrock of the Rio Piedras, Senor Shadmer."

CHAPTER IX.

The Phantom Sheriff averted his head as he spurred past the Mexican outpost. The sentinel put fingers to lips and gave a low, penetrating whistle, followed by an owl's hoot.

From up ahead on the rocky slope of Cartridge Peak came an answering signal, and Spook Sidlaw knew that the smugglers would be awaiting his arrival.

A hundred yards farther on, Sidlaw arrived at a small brush corral, in which several horses were standing. A squatty Mexican approached him as he reined up and dismounted.

"*Como 'sta*, Senor Shadmer?" greeted the Mexican.

"*Bien*." The Phantom Sheriff was thankful for the Spanish he had picked up during the time he had knocked around the border cow camps. He would stand in need of that knowledge tonight.

Turning his reins over to the coral keeper, Sidlaw headed in the direction of the smuggler's camp. He loosened his six-guns in holsters as he walked, breathing a silent prayer of thanks that the smugglers had no campfire.

Quirly butts glowed and ebbed like the red eyes of crouched panthers as Sidlaw walked up, his gaze sweeping a ring of squatting men. Five of them were grouped in a circle about two hombres who were seated on a big rock in the center.

One of the pair the Phantom Sheriff recognized by the shape of his sombrero as Pancho Pedro, the messenger who had accosted him in Smoketree that night. The other was smoking a Mexican cigarette whose glow revealed a brown face deeply scarred with smallpox pits.

Sidlaw squatted on the outer edge of the circle, acknowledging greetings with non-committal grunts. His eyes slanted under the pulled-down brim of his Stetson to study the pock-marked Mexie. Instinctively he knew this must be Francisco Yuma, ace smuggler.

"*Hola*, Senor Gila Jack!" came the low, hard voice of the outlaw chief. "Pancho Pedro here tells me he had a hard time finding you in Smoketree, senor. He was told at your cantina that you ambushed the gringo sheriff today. *Verdad*?"

Rage flooded Sidlaw at this confirmation of his hunch that Gila Jack Shadmer had been Buck Clawson's dry-gulcher on the street following the attempted holdup of the Border State Bank.

"*Si*," returned the Phantom Sheriff, thankful that the smugglers were conversing in such low tones that it enabled him to imitate Shadmer's voice without undue risk of detection. "The sheriff is *morte*—dead."

Mutters of excitement and congratulations rippled around the circle of smugglers at this news.

"The ol' tin-star died, eh, Shadmer?" came an American voice from the far edge of the ring of men. "Good work, Jack. It took yuh a plumb long time to salivate Clawson, but now that yuh've done it, I reckon yuh got Malpais County by the tail on a downhill pull, eh?"

"Yeah," seconded another gringo voice. "Congratulations, Gila Jack. Say, Yuma—how about lightin' a fire? My bones is plumb achin' from the cold. If Buck Clawson is croaked, an' all o' his depities turned in their badges like Pancho Pedro told us when he got back from Smoketree tonight, I don't see no need o' us hunkerin' hyar like coyotes, freezin'."

Francisco Yuma shook his head.

"For the benefit of you amigos from Nogales who have not met with us before," rasped the outlaw boss, speaking in Spanish, "I will tell you that the reason we have never failed in our smuggling across the Border is because we are as careful as the wild lobo in everything we do. We build no fires to reveal our meeting place to other eyes, Senor Carson."

The gringo addressed as Carson grunted.

"O.K. But supposin' we divide up that opium an' be driftin' our picket pins, chief. It's a long ride back to Huachuca, an' I want to be leavin'.

78

Now that Gila Jack's arrived, I reckon we're all here an' kin start business."

There was a shifting of feet as the smugglers arose and stretched. In the dim starlight, Spook Sidlaw saw Yuma lift the lid from a wooden powder box and draw out a tin can.

"This shipment of opium I am selling you at one hundred pesos per can tonight, *compadres*," announced Francisco Yuma.

A mutter of dissent circled the smugglers.

"A hundred pesos?" protested Carson angrily. "Yuh only soaked us eighty last month, Yuma. What's the idea raisin' the ante thisaway? Yuh're lucky we risk our hides to buy yore stuff at all."

Yuma shrugged.

"Yeah—ain't it risky enough gittin' this dope acrost the line to American markets," protested another voice, "without you boostin' the price every month, Yuma?"

Francisco Yuma dropped the can back in the powder box.

"No one has to buy, Senor Lockery. After all, you are getting rich selling my opium up in the mining camps and over in Nogales, *no es verdad*? Where else could you get opium, amigo, except from me? I am the only smuggler on this part of the border—"

Men cursed futilely and Sidlaw heard money jangle as the smugglers drew pokes and wallets from their pockets.

Excitement made the Phantom Sheriff's heart race. He had come to this outlaw meeting with no definite idea of how the notorious Francisco Yuma worked. He realized, now, that it would be impossible for him to make a wholesale capture of the villainous gang who were trafficking in contraband dope and the human misery it entailed.

But, by keeping his ears open, he had picked up plenty of knowledge since his arrival. Evidently Yuma obtained the illegal drugs somewhere in old Mexico, after which he met gringo buyers at this prearranged hide-out south of the American line, out of reach of American law.

The gringos would pay Yuma's price for the opium and then resell it in Arizona, probably at a profit of several hundred percent. And, according to what hearsay accounts Sidlaw remembered concerning Francisco Yuma, the clever Mexican had been smuggling successfully for years.

"You win, Yuma," grumbled Carson. "I kin use six cans this month. Them chinks up at the minin' camps want it bad—even at yore prices."

A shuffling Mexican whom Sidlaw recognized as Pancho Pedro, the messenger who had accosted him at Smoketree earlier in the evening, proceeded to hand out tin cans of opium to the smugglers assembled about them.

Coins clinked and greenbacks crackled, as money changed hands. In each case, Francisco

Yuma inspected the dinero carefully by the reflected glow of his cigarette butt. Evidently very little trust was being shown on either side.

The cold fingers of dread clamped about Spook Sidlaw's heart as he felt in his pocket and found the lone twenty-dollar gold piece which was all the cash he had in the world.

Twenty dollars would probably not buy a fraction of the opium which Gila Jack Shadmer was in the habit of purchasing from Francisco Yuma every month.

When the moment came for him to buy cans of contraband drugs from Pancho Pedro, he would have no excuse to offer for not having brought enough money along to pay for the transaction.

That would force a showdown, and the Phantom Sheriff knew he was in no position to tip his hand as yet.

Even if he were able to gun down the ringleader of the smugglers, he knew that a dozen guns would riddle him with slugs before he could possibly reach his horse at the brush corral down the mountainside.

Already the other smugglers had obtained their quota of opium and were packing the cans in saddlebags. Pancho Pedro approached Sidlaw as the waddy squatted in the darkness, palms tensed on gun butts.

"*Quantos*, Senor Shadmer—how many?" demanded Pancho Pedro, halting in front of the Phantom Sheriff.

Before Sidlaw could frame a reply, the night was suddenly shattered by a hoarse bellow of the Mexican sentinel down the slope. It was followed by the report of a rifle.

Instantly on the heels of the .30-30 explosion a six-gun thundered twice in rapid succession. The agonized squall of the mortally wounded Mexican lookout died on the night wind.

"*Caramba*!" yelled Francisco Yuma, snatching a Winchester that had leaned against the boulder. "Someone has attacked Dominguez!"

Hoofbeats rattled up the slope as the smugglers jerked six-guns from holsters and raced for the shelter of boulders, to await the arrival of the man who had shot their sentinel.

"*Hola*, the camp!" came a hoarse yell from the approaching horseman. "What in blazes is goin' on tonight, anyhow? First you don't send me the password like you wrote me you would, an' then Dominguez cuts loose with his .30-30 when I ride up an' tell him who I am!"

Francisco Yuma, kneeling behind his sheltering boulder with cocked rifle resting on the rocky parapet, snarled out an oath.

"Who comes?" he challenged as the mounted man loomed up against the skyline and sat his saddle, staring down at the camp. "No one else was expected tonight. If you come, you are an enemy!"

A torrent of gringo profanity followed Yuma's demand.

"Me an enemy—when I been dealin' with you longer'n anybody else in yore gang?" roared the newcomer in a voice which turned the Phantom Sheriff's heart to ice. "You was expectin' me, warn't yuh? Since when do you make an enemy o' Gila Jack Shadmer?"

CHAPTER X.

There was a moment of frozen silence as the smugglers digested the rider's startling announcement.

Gila Jack Shadmer sensed the tension, but misunderstood its cause.

"I know we're supposed to give a password tonight on account o' some new men meetin' with us," apologized the Smoketree gambler, "but when Pancho Pedro didn't show up an' I knew we was supposed to meet tonight, I jest come on up an'—"

A startled yell came from Carson hiding behind a boulder a dozen yards from the spot where Spook Sidlaw crouched, six-guns in hand, waiting for the inevitable showdown to break.

"That's Jack Shadmer, all right, chief! I know that voice!"

The gringo named Lockery demanded, with a catch of panic in his voice: "Then who in blazes is that busky who gave us the password an' claimed *he* was Gila Jack?"

Francisco Yuma swung his rifle about, beady eyes searching the thick gloom for a glimpse of the impostor. And Spook Sidlaw moved fast, in the split second of time in which he knew the smuggler chief would be figuring out his location.

With a cougarlike spring, the Phantom Sheriff headed for a bubble-pitted lava boulder a dozen feet away. Even as he did so the ear-shattering report of Yuma's .30-30 blasted the night.

The whistling breath of the missile whipped Sidlaw's neck as he leaped for the sheltering rock.

Then he gasped with horror as he found the muzzle of Pancho Pedro's six-gun inches from his face, the Mexican's villainous countenance twisted in a leer of hate as he eared back the hammer.

At point-blank range, the Phantom Sheriff jerked triggers of both his six-guns before Pancho Pedro could shoot.

Converging slugs ripped through the half-breed's neck, spinning him backward and flopping him dead on the flinty earth.

With a startled yell, Gila Jack Shadmer vaulted out of his saddle and landed behind the boulder where his friend, Francisco Yuma, was crouching.

"What is this, Yuma?" cried Gila Jack Shadmer, drawing his own guns as he squatted shoulder to shoulder by the smuggling chief. "What'd Rib Carson an' Jed Lockery say about somebody givin' the password an' claimin' to be me?"

Francisco Yuma peered over the boulder, then ducked as Spook Sidlaw, firing from behind the rock where Pancho Pedro had hidden, triggered a slug through the high cone of his ball-tasseled sombrero.

"*Es verdad*, Senor Shadmer. Someone treeked us tonight. I thought you were weeth us. But eet was not you—eet was an impostor. I make the bad mistake, *si*."

Sidlaw raked the gloom with shuttling eyes and weaving gun barrels. His position was spotted now; and the slaying of Pancho Pedro would incense these smugglers to fever pitch. Once they surrounded him, Sidlaw knew his finish would be swift and bloody.

Icy sweat oozed from his pores as he sighted a beeline down the slope toward the brush corral where his horse waited. It was open ground, without so much as a bush to hide behind.

It would be impossible to reach the corral alive. Yet he knew he could not linger many moments behind this rock, where he had gunned Pancho Pedro into eternity.

Once the smugglers overcame their confusion at discovering a spy in camp, they would fling a circle about him and wait for daylight to enable them to gun him down. Nothing would give this case-hardened gang more pleasure than using a lawman's badge for a target, Sidlaw knew.

"Who was this hombre?" came Gila Jack Shadmer's startled voice. "Who was it? How'd he git the password?"

Francisco Yuma shrugged.

"*Quien sabe.* Pancho Pedro ees dead, or perhaps we could find out. I am the fool that I do not look at each man's face carefully instead of depending on thos' password. Whoever eet ees beyond that rock, he ees a very brave hombre, *es seguro.*"

The Phantom Sheriff heard spur chains tinkling as other smugglers crawled closer. Every man hiding behind the pall of darkness knew that the impostor in their midst must not be allowed to escape. Otherwise the smuggling ring would never be able to use Cartridge Peak for a rendezvous again.

"Listen, amigos!" yelled Shadmer, taking charge of the situation in which he found himself the key figure. "Whoever this yahoo is, he's got to be salivated pronto. Mebbe it's another one o' them U. S. marshals, who got the password from Pancho Pedro by a ruse. Anyhow, we know he's hunkerin' behind that boulder. So we might as well go to work!"

Sidlaw took advantage of the moment's silence to eject empty shells from his hot-barreled Colts and reload from the ammunition in his cartridge-belt loops. Again he scanned the open slope separating him from the remuda of saddle horses. Whatever chance he had of making an open break was gone now. Again Shadmer's yell rang out sharply:

"Listen, Rib Carson! You, Jed Lockery—an' you new fellers from Nogales. Yuh hear me?"

Cautious grunts from various points along the hillside, above and behind Spook Sidlaw, answered the gambler.

"Belly down an' circle that rock. If that jigger comes out in the open, me an' Yuma will tally him from here. If he don't, you fellers kin draw a bead on him next time the clouds break an' let a little light through!"

Even as he spoke, a taunting fate ignited a sheet of yellow heat-lightning along the clouds nesting beyond the stony shoulders of Cartridge Peak. In the pinched-off interval of light, Sidlaw caught sight of the skulking figures of his besiegers as they crawled like reptiles along the slope, aiming to cut him off from escape.

Another flash of lightning, weak and remote as it was, would give them ample light to notch their gun-sights on him.

And the two kingpins of the smuggling ring whom Sidlaw wanted to tally before he himself was gunned down—Francisco Yuma and Gila Jack Shadmer—would make sure that they did not leave the protection of their own boulder.

"No use lettin' 'em crawl any closer," decided the Phantom Sheriff grimly as he got to his knees. "Mebbe I kin make a dash fer them ponies, fork one of 'em an' stampede the rest. I ain't got the chance of a snowball in Hades, but it beats squattin' hyar an' lettin' 'em take their time about killin' me."

Tensing his muscles for action, Spook Sidlaw bounded to a running posture like a sprinter starting a race.

The rattle of his slogging boots was the signal for an ear-stunning burst of gunfire from several points, and bullets kicked gravel about his legs as Sidlaw fled down the hillside in the direction of the cavvy corral.

In the darkness, shooting at a rapidly-moving target was difficult. On that lone factor, Sidlaw banked his scant chances.

A running outlaw veered in from a brushy thicket to his left, and Sidlaw thumbed a bullet across his midriff as he ran.

A gagged scream came from Rib Carson as the gringo pursuer collapsed, to lay writhing on the ground, fingers clawing feebly at a spouting bullet hole in his side.

The roar of six-guns and the harsher explosion of Francisco Yuma's .30-30 resounded in the sheriff's ear as he sprinted for the corral at top speed, hoping against hope that he would not trip on the loose stones underfoot.

A slug tore a slot in his bat-wing chaps. Another snapped a spur rowel from its shank on his left boot, the concussion knocking him sprawling, only to pick himself up, recover a fallen six-gun and race on down the hillside.

Running figures charged after him, ghostly in the darkness, zigzagging to avoid return gunfire.

Then, as Sidlaw skidded to a halt alongside the brush corral, he saw a Colt spit fire not ten feet away. It was the *mozo* in charge of the remuda.

Flinging himself sideways into the scant protection of the brush fence, the Phantom Sheriff levelled both guns at the Mexican hostler who stood spread-legged, guarding the corral gate.

Sidlaw's .45 bucked and roared in his left hand. The night breeze whipped fumes away from the Colt muzzle and showed him the sickening sight of the dead *mozo*, face drilled by tunneling lead, keeling over against the fence.

Sidlaw holstered the gun, then hunted for and found the rail forming the gate of the crude pen. He flung it aside, rushed to the nearest horse in the milling remuda.

Out from his shelter emerged Gila Jack Shadmer, as another sheet of lightning illuminated the smoky scene for an instant.

"After him, pards! He's vamoosin'!"

Shadmer vaulted into his own saddle at the same instant that the Phantom Sheriff seized a trailing bridle rein, wedged boot to stirrup, and swung aboard a horse he had taken at random from the half a dozen mounts in the corral.

"*Andale*, pards!" came the gambler's bellow as he wheeled his own horse in pursuit. "He must 'a' croaked Manuel an' is choosin' one o' yore hosses!"

Sidlaw spurred his mount sharply, trusting to luck that the pony he had chosen would be able to clear the brush fence on the downhill side of the corral.

He pitched forward in the saddle as the boogery mount balked on the verge of the hurdle, but momentum carried the animal against the flimsy barrier and crashed on through without losing its footing.

Down the dim trail the Phantom Sheriff spurred, his heart bounding with the first glimmer of hope he had had since the unforeseen and disastrous appearance of the real Gila Jack Shadmer.

Plastered Indian fashion over his bronc's withers, the escaping waddy peered back up the rocky slope of Cartridge Peak and snapped a shot at the oncoming figure of Shadmer.

The Smoketree saloonman, elbows bobbing, was rapidly overtaking him. Hoofbeats clattered on the rocks back at the camp, as Francisco Yuma and the assembled smugglers fought desperately to grab the reins of their own panicked horses.

Wind whipped Sidlaw's face. A lightning flicker showed him the black gulf of the dry coulee ahead of him, and he spurred toward it, recklessly disregarding the roughness of the trail.

He got a blurred glimpse of the dead sentinel, Dominguez, who had challenged Jack Shadmer and lost his own life.

Twisting in the saddle, Sidlaw steadied his right wrist with his free hand, seeking to draw a bead on the fast-approaching figure of Gila Jack Shadmer.

Even as he squeezed trigger, his pony went down as a hoof wedged into a rocky fissure on the trail.

The saddlehorn raked the Phantom Sheriff's leg as he was hurled free of the saddle, to land with a resounding thump on a bed of dry thistle poppies.

Reeling to his feet in a shower of stars, Spook Sidlaw tried to bring up his guns as Gila Jack Shadmer charged him with the chestnut that had belonged to Freddie Clawson.

Crash! The horse's left foreleg hurled Sidlaw to one side as he sought to avoid the oncoming animal.

Rolling like a flung stick, the cowboy sprawled limp and sick on the ground, unable to get up as Gila Jack Shadmer reined his horse about and leaped from the saddle, leveling his Colt .45 for the payoff shot at close range.

With a gasp of horror and pain, Sidlaw rolled dazedly aside in time to avoid Shadmer's bullet.

Even as the gambler's slug pounded the rocks near his head and whined off into the night sky, the Phantom Sheriff relaxed in merciful unconsciousness, his heavy-lidded eyes staring at the scudding clouds.

CHAPTER XI.

Francisco Yuma galloped up on his own flaxen-tailed palomino, reining to a dusty halt as he saw that Gila Jack had brought down their enemy.

Farther back up Cartridge Peak, the remainder of the smuggling gang had succeeded in mounting horses and were belatedly joining the chase.

Horsemen formed a ring about the squatting figure of Gila Jack Shadmer as the gambler thumbed flame from a match and held it above their captive's contorted face. Then, before the match flickered out, he stooped closer to study the engraved words on Sidlaw's solid-gold badge.

"I'll be danged," whispered the gun boss of Smoketree in an awed tone. "Gents, this ain't no stranger who tried to fill my boots tonight. It's a waddy who drifted into Smoketree yesterday mornin' just after I'd ambushed the sheriff."

The outlaws stared down at the groaning figure. "Whoever he is, Jack," spoke up Jed Lockery, "he's a John Law. I kin see his badge from here!"

Shadmer nodded, a puzzled frown on his brow.

"He ain't a U. S. marshal. He's the Phantom Sheriff."

Francisco Yuma paled behind his saddle-colored skin.

"The Phantom Sheriff? From Texas? Thees ees *muy malo*."

The other outlaws shuddered in spite of themselves as they repeated the name which owl-hoot riders held in dread.

"But what would the Phantom Sheriff be doin' hyar on Ca'tridge Peak?" demanded one of the new smugglers from Nogales. "His home range is east o' the Pecos, I thought."

Gila Jack Shadmer fingered a waxed mustache tip as he stared at the body of the man he had trailed up to Buck Clawson's house that night.

"I think I kin explain the set-up," mused the Smoketree killer. "I've heard it rumored that the Phantom Sheriff is the fightin' whelp o' old Buck Clawson. The sheriff sent fer him to clean up Smoketree, like he cleaned up them towns along the Rio Grande. It'd be plumb nacheral that the first thing this Phantom Sheriff would do would be to try an' put a kibosh on our smugglin', jest like Buck Clawson tried to do fer so long."

A satisfied grin creased Shadmer's brutal visage. Back in Smoketree, a courageous girl had saved the Phantom Sheriff's life. The opportune arrival of Doc Frazer had forced Shadmer to flee.

But now things were different. They were on the desolate slope of Cartridge Peak. And because he himself had just ridden up from Smoketree, Jack Shadmer was positive that the

Phantom Sheriff had not brought a posse up to the smugglers' rendezvous.

"Thees Phantom Sheriff," said Francisco Yuma with a voice that plainly betrayed his fears, "ees *muy malo*. We must keel heem *ahora*—right now, Senor Shadmer."

Gila Jack Shadmer stepped over to his horse and unbuckled a pleated rawhide riata from the swell-fork pommel.

"I'm goin' to kill the Phantom Sheriff," he said grimly, "but in my own way. In such a way that he'll know, before he dies, that the hombre he come out from Texas to buck was a shade too salty fer him to handle. An' I aim to kill him in such a way that his body'll never be found if anybody investigates."

Rolling Spook Sidlaw over on his back, Shadmer proceeded to tie the waddy's wrists together and then bind his arms tightly to his sides.

That done, Shadmer returned to his horse and unlooped a canvas canteen from the cantle.

The smugglers stared curiously at the gambler as Gila Jack poured the icy contents of the water bag over Sidlaw's hair and face.

Sputtering and groaning, the Phantom Sheriff stirred as the water revived his dazed senses.

So engrossed was Shadmer in his work that he and the other Border hoppers failed to hear the sound of approaching hoofbeats until a lone rider spurred his mount out of the dry coulee fifty yards down the ridge.

"Watch out, boys—trouble comin'!"

Shadmer snaked a .45 from leather, Yuma and the opium runners following suit as they made out the form of the approaching horseman.

"Rein up!" yelled Gila Jack, his own Colts trained on the rider. "Who is it?"

A gruff voice answered him:

"Yore bartender, Curly Bardoo. Don't shoot, boys!"

Shadmer relaxed, giving a gruff order through tight lips:

"Close-hobble yore shootin' irons, boys. Bardoo's O.K. Must be somethin' wrong in Smoketree to send him kitin' up hyar."

The pot-bellied saloonkeeper from the Lucky Dollars dismounted and led his horse up to the group.

"What brings you out here, Curly?" demanded Shadmer. "Ain't I told you never to foller me to these smugglin' meetin's? The rest o' the boys don't like it."

Curly Bardoo nodded apologetically.

"I know, chief. But thar's hell to pay back in Smoketree. I rid out hyar to warn yuh not to show up in town after daylight, Gila Jack."

The gambler scowled uncertainly.

"Make *habla*, Bardoo. What's happen in town to throw you in a lather thisaway?"

The bartender jerked a thumb in the direction of Smoketree.

"The whole town's up in arms when they heard about the sheriff kickin' off, Jack. Doc Frazer spilt the beans about you bein' his killer. A riot like to busted out in the Lucky Dollars Saloon, when the news got around. I had to close the place fer fear they'd bust things up. Soon as I could, I lit a shuck out here to warn yuh not to come back to town till things blow over."

Shadmer sneered contemptuously at the bartender's excitement.

"Settle yoreself, Bardoo. Reckon I ramrodded that burg when Buck Clawson was lawin' thar. Why should I git spooky now that the sheriff's headed fer boothill? Reckon we'll be top dog in Smoketree from now on."

Curly Bardoo shook his head desperately.

"But thar's a new set-up in Smoketree tonight, chief. I don't like the looks of it. Never seed the town so riled. Women an' storekeepers an' even the Mexican kids was heavin' rocks at our windows when I burned hosshair to git here."

"But why? How come they're stampedin' this-away?"

"They're sayin' they're goin' to string you up, Jack, fer murderin' Buck Clawson. I reckon yore reign in Smoketree town is done fer keeps, chief."

Shadmer laughed. "You mean it's jest startin'."

It was the first time since Shadmer had put Smoketree under the menace of his gun-slinging crew that he had heard signs of rebellion, but Bardoo's fear left him cold.

"Yuh see, Jack," continued the bartender, "Smoketree knows that this Phantom Sheriff has arrived to fight their battles fer 'em. Doc Frazer told 'em this Phantom Sheriff had tamed wilder places than Smoketree, an' that the Phantom Sheriff would have yore hide curin' on a fence rail inside a week!"

CHAPTER XII.

Francisco Yuma and his gang joined in the gambler's derisive laugh as Curly Bardoo revealed the cause behind Smoketree's rebellion against Shadmer's gun rule.

"Is that so, Bardoo?" jeered the gambler, turning to point down at the groaning figure of Spook Sidlaw.

"Waal, drop yore eyes on this bronc-twister here, Bardoo. He's the Phantom Sheriff. He got proddy tonight an' figgered he could smash Yuma's smugglin' ring, an' me along with it. Yuh see how far he got."

"Poleax me fer a heifer, Gila Jack!" cried the barkeep admiringly. "I might 'a' known you'd dab yore loop on that Phantom Sheriff feller if he tried rammin' his horns into yuh."

Shadmer stooped and seized Spook Sidlaw by the armpits. With a grunting effort he lifted the dazed waddy to his feet, and Francisco Yuma stepped forward to help support the sheriff's weight.

Shaking his head doggedly to rid his brain of the red fireworks which hampered his vision, Spook Sidlaw stared first at the gambler on his right, then at Francisco Yuma.

"I heard yore booger talk jest now, Shadmer,"

he panted, his skull aching as if a live coal were embedded in the spot where Shadmer's horse had struck his scalp. "But yore bartender told yuh right. Smoketree's got a bellyful o' yore bullyin' it into an owl-hoot town."

"Yeah?"

"They don't need no Phantom Sheriff to lead 'em, Shadmer. They'll be stringin' you up same as they threatened to do tonight. Killin' me won't stop 'em. They'll git revenge fer Buck Clawson's murder. Yuh're finished, Shadmer."

The gambler snarled and rocked his captive's head with a stinging slap to the cheek.

"You talk right salty fer a jasper who ain't got but about two more minutes to brag, feller!" snarled the gambler. "Come on, Yuma. We're headin' fer the canyon o' the Rio Piedras."

Stumbling helplessly, his body dragged along by the boss smuggler and Gila Jack Shadmer, the Phantom Sheriff felt himself being hauled southward.

Behind him, Curly Bardoo and the smugglers followed curiously.

It was typical of Gila Jack Shadmer's ruthless nature that he should figure out some horrible way to put an end to his helpless enemy, and in spite of themselves the smugglers decided to remain on Cartridge Peak long enough to witness the Phantom Sheriff's end.

Fifty feet ahead, a dark split broke the rocky

terrain—a chasm whose rims were furred with cactus and weeds. As they neared the yawning gulf there came to Sidlaw's ears the low rumble of water cascading over the rocky throat of the canyon, far below.

Reaching the brink of the cliff, the outlaws lined up on the rimrock, shuddering in spite of themselves.

The roar of the Rio Piedras churning over its jagged, rocky bed sounded as sinister in their ears as the roar of a wild beast.

"You will put a bullet in his head and throw him in the river, Senor Shadmer?" Yuma addressed Shadmer in Mexican, his breath foul against the side of Spook's neck.

Shadmer's laugh made Sidlaw recoil in horror.

"I'm shovin' him over this cliff, yes," replied the Smoketree outlaw. "But on the way down he's goin' to be alive. Afore he smashes to hash-meat on them rocks a hundred foot down thar below Silver Falls, I reckon the Phantom Sheriff will have time to regret he didn't keep his picket pin in Texas."

Thoughts raced through Sidlaw's brain. Terror left him, to be replaced by a consuming sense of bitterness—regret for the fate of the innocent folk of Malpais County, doomed to feel the oppression of this merciless criminal.

His role as the Phantom Sheriff was winding up in tragedy, less than twenty-four hours after his arrival in Buck Clawson's town. He had accomplished exactly nothing, he reminded himself bitterly.

Memory of Marie Clawson's trust in him taunted the cowboy, as he felt Gila Jack Shadmer's iron fingers push against his shoulder blades as he stood on the lip of the gorge.

Marie had had faith in him, a faith that had caused her to pin her brother's gold badge on his shirt. He had failed. He found himself wondering, with a sickish feeling of hopelessness, whether Freddie Clawson would have succeeded in his grim mission had he not been cut down by an ambush bullet from Gila Jack Shadmer.

"It's adios fer you, I reckon, Phantom Sheriff!" grated the outlaw. "I reckon I'm glad, now, that I didn't git to blow out yore brains at the sheriff's house tonight!"

So saying, Shadmer leaned back, then shoved the wabbly-legged cowboy in the small of the back.

Propelled out into black, empty nothingness, the Phantom Sheriff felt himself plummeting down, down, down through sickening space to vanish in the pounding spray of Silver Falls.

CHAPTER XIII.

Plummeting dizzily through spray-clouded space, Spook Sidlaw had a blurring glimpse of the tumbling white cascade of Silver Falls as a sliver of lightning blazed in the sky above the rimrock of Rio Piedras Canyon.

Spray stung his checks like driving pebbles during the incredibly short time it took his hurtling body to drop another fifty feet.

Then a roiling caldron of icy water rushed up to meet him. His boot-clad legs dropped into the foamy wash as if he had intentionally dived feet-first from the cliff ledge far above.

The thunder of plunging tons of water drowned the sound of his dive, as the river closed over his head in an icy rush.

Some ironic quirk of fate kept Sidlaw conscious, expecting each split second to feel the impact of the jagged rocks, which the outlaws had said formed the pit of the canyon.

But, instead of rocks, only deep, unplumbed water met his plunge!

Momentum carried him down, otterlike, through twenty feet that served as a slow, cushioning brake for his dive.

Then the surging, U-shaped current formed by

Silver Falls overcame the force of gravity and began leveling his body out.

Helpless to churn the water with his arms because of the rawhide bonds which held his elbows and wrists to his body, Sidlaw could do nothing. But instinct, the sheer will of a man to live, closed his lips and nostrils against the pressure of the icy water, keeping it out of his lungs.

Like a chip in a maelstrom, he felt conflicting currents tear at his body with icy fingers, even as his knees and hips came into jarring contact with the bowlike smoothness which marked the bottom of the deep pool. The tumbling waterfall had spent untold centuries in gouging this out.

Buffeting side currents seized the Phantom Sheriff's body, rolled him roughly over smooth, curving stone. Then the upward rush of water overcame the weight of his cartridge belts and bat-wing chaps and heavy cow boots, and Sidlaw shot upward.

Lungs seemingly exploding within him for want of oxygen, he struggled to keep from sucking river water into his windpipe, until his head broke the surface of the waterfall's pool in a roil of foam.

Pounding cascades overhead once more plunged him into chill depths, but not before he had expelled the used air from his lungs and sucked deeply again.

When he broke the surface of the Rio Piedras next, twisting currents had carried him to the rock-toothed edge of the pool, which was eternally invisible from above due to the steamlike clouds of spray which clogged the narrow gorge.

Sluicing water carried him twice around the dizzy whirlpool. Then Sidlaw's rawhide-trussed body was tumbled roughly out on a bed of jagged rocks in the stream channel proper.

Only the fact that tough bullhide chaps covered his legs had prevented him from receiving crippling bruises.

Limp and exhausted, the Phantom Sheriff found himself in three feet of water, his body hammered mercilessly by the foaming millrace above the rapids.

No longer was he in deep water under the falls. At any instant the plunging torrent might sweep him into the boulder-fanged bed of the river.

His legs were not bound. His strength revived by the icy water, the Phantom Sheriff waded desperately through the spray-choked darkness.

Sluicing currents assisted him. A few moments later he crawled through the shallow waters edging the river to collapse unconscious on a muddy sand bar.

How long he lay there, Spook Sidlaw never knew. But, when consciousness once more returned to him, he was aware of the ear-deafening din of the waterfall behind him, and of the numbing temperature of the water in which his legs still rested.

With feeble, toadlike kicks Sidlaw pushed himself farther up on the shelf of sand and gravel until he no longer felt the sinister tug of the current on his boot-clad ankles.

For a long time he lay gasping like a landed trout, as his thoughts gradually adjusted themselves inside his throbbing skull.

Not until then did he realize what had saved him from certain death after Gila Jack Shadmer had hurled him off the rimrock a hundred feet above.

"They figgered I'd land on these rocks," muttered the cowboy, shuddering convulsively from the cold. "Instead, I landed in that deep hole the falls had wore *out* o' the rocks. Lucky that pool was deep, after a dive like that!"

Daylight must be close at hand, he figured, for a peach-colored glow was suffusing the spray-choked canyon of the Rio Piedras. His straining eyes could see Silver Falls from its bottom to its crest. Sheer, beetling cliffs soared overhead, seemingly supporting the Mexican sky.

A sixth sense warned him that he might be visible from above in case any of the outlaws on Cartridge Peak chanced to peer down into the canyon in search of his mangled corpse.

Groaning with the effort, Spook Sidlaw wriggled his way into a dense thicket of water grass and scrub tornillo, and once more slumped with exhaustion.

A ruddy sun was just slanting its first rays down the canyon when Spook sat up once more. The roar of the waterfall fifty yards away was so intense he could hardly think, but he was aware of one heartening thing—the braided Mexican lariat which bound his arms had seemingly loosened for the dull pain of strained muscles and ligaments in arms and shoulder blades had eased up.

"Rawhide stretches when it gits wet!" the cowboy mused, new hope surging through his body making him forget the ache of bruised sinews and sore bones. "Mebbe thar's a chance I won't stay hogtied fer long, after all!"

He tugged at his left arm. A glow of triumph swept over him as he felt his wrist disengage itself from swollen, slippery rawhide bonds. A moment later it tugged free.

By wriggling his body against the stubby willows, he managed to unkink an elbow and slowly free his left arm from the snakelike coils of wet riata.

Once he had one hand to work with, Sidlaw made short work of disengaging his other arm. Then, standing up groggily, he pulled the wet coils of rope down his hips and legs and stepped out of his bonds.

He was standing in shoulder-high brush. In

the rays of the rising sun, he inspected himself carefully for broken bones and was relieved to find none.

Aside from the flesh wound on his scalp, caused by Gila Jack Shadmer riding him down on horseback, he had escaped serious injury in the melee on Cartridge Peak.

"But I ain't out o' the woods yet, by a long shot!" muttered the Wyoming puncher as he untied the knots in the lariat and coiled it over his arm. "Gittin' out o' this canyon may not be easy fer an hombre as stove-up an' tired out as I feel."

He peered anxiously down the canyon. Flooding tons of water sluiced down the rocks, presenting an unending series of terraced rapids which he knew no man, however fit, could possibly cross without fatal injury or drowning.

Once those racing currents seized him, Sidlaw knew he would be dashed to his death on the series of smaller waterfalls.

He turned his attention to the cliffs, noting with approval that they did not present a sheer, unscalable front. Instead, the canyon walls were broken up with ledges and shelves, dotted with frequent brush clumps which might offer a handhold.

Seating himself on a mossy boulder, the Phantom Sheriff tugged off his boots and emptied the water from them. Wringing out his socks, he next squeezed as much water as possible from his red-checkered shirt.

The grateful warmth of the morning sun slowly tempered the chill air of Rio Piedras Canyon. With warmth came a flexing of his bruised muscles, and Sidlaw knew he was at least physically ready for his attempted climb to freedom.

"Lucky the current beached me on the north side," he mused, starting up the first brushy slope toward the cliff bottom. "Otherwise I couldn't 'a' crossed the river."

The slope took him fifty feet above the river level, or more than halfway up the cliff's face.

Then a twenty-foot sheer wall seemingly blocked his progress, but Spook Sidlaw hadn't been bred on a cow range for nothing. Shaking out a loop in the Mexican riata which Gila Jack Shadmer had used in trussing him the night before, the cowboy cast the noose at a projecting knob of rock at the rim of the next higher ledge.

Successful after a half dozen tries, he scrambled hand-over-hand to the grassy shelf.

Then, unlooping the rope from the projecting rock, Sidlaw started the relatively easy ascent to the rimrock which stood sharp-etched against the cloudless Mexican sky.

"I got to take it easy, in case Shadmer an' them smugglers o' his are still in camp," thought the waddy when he had climbed to within a dozen feet of the rim. "I'd be in a purty kettle o' fish if I blundered right back into their hands."

Crawling cautiously, he snaked his way to a hedge of ignota and wild tobacco brush on the rimrock.

His caution had not been ill-advised. Even as he peered through the thick foliage for a view of the sun-drenched slope of Cartridge Peak, Spook Sidlaw caught sight of his foemen.

Not fifty feet away, Gila Jack Shadmer and Francisco Yuma were busily engaged in dragging four dead men toward a hole which they had evidently scraped out of the gravel during the final hours of the night.

Sidlaw recognized the four bullet-riddled corpses as victims of the night's battle. There was Dominguez, the sentinel whom Shadmer had slain when he arrived at the smugglers' meeting.

Another dead Mexican was the *mozo* whom Sidlaw had been forced to kill at the gate of the brush corral. A red-whiskered corpse was evidently Rib Carson, whom he had shot during his wild effort at a getaway. The fourth body was that of the messenger and Yuma's henchman, Pancho Pedro.

Of the other smugglers there was no trace; evidently they had pouched their opium supply and ridden back to their home ranges, immediately after seeing the Phantom Sheriff hurled to what seemed inevitable doom.

A thrill coursed through the Phantom Sheriff as he noticed that Yuma and the gambler were burying their dead henchmen without bothering to dispossess the corpses of their guns or cartridge belts.

Sidlaw knew he would find a use for those buried firearms, once he emerged from hiding.

CHAPTER XIV.

When they had finished their grisly work of burying the night's gunshot victims, Francisco Yuma and Gila Jack Shadmer walked back up the mountainside to the nearby camp.

Shadmer's horse—the chestnut which had belonged to Freddie Clawson—was tied to the brush fence of the open corral. Nearby was a flaxen-tailed palamino bearing a Chihuahua brand which evidently was Francisco Yuma's mount.

"If only I could lay my hands on a smoke pole right now, I reckon thar'd be two more dead skunks to bury this mornin'!" muttered the Phantom Sheriff as he lay prone in his brushy hide-out on the canyon brink. "But all I kin do is bide my time, I reckon."

As the two smugglers saddled up for their departure, Spook Sidlaw caught Shadmer's voice raised in exultation.

"Not a bad night's work, Francisco," boomed the Smoketree saloonman as he mounted the chestnut. "I'm sorry about Pancho Pedro gittin' salivated, but I reckon we're lucky the Phantom Sheriff didn't plug us. He was a salty one."

Francisco Yuma adjusted the chin strap of his big sombrero and nodded somberly as he leaned from the saddle to shake his *compadre*'s hand in farewell.

"Een thees business we must accept theengs as they come, no?" said Yuma. "Adios for now, amigo. Een one month from today we meet here for another opium shipment, *si*?"

The two talked for a few minutes in voices too low for the hidden sheriff to overhear. Then Gila Jack Shadmer reared his stolen mount and headed down the trail toward Smoketree, so close to Sidlaw's hiding place that he could see the redhot streaks in Shadmer's eyes.

Francisco Yuma spurred his palomino westward, and fifteen minutes later they vanished over the skyline, bound for the interior of the Sonora province.

The Phantom Sheriff waited until he saw Gila Jack disappear down the coulee trail toward Smoketree. Then he emerged from hiding.

A brief survey of the smugglers' camp revealed to him that there were no firearms left lying about. Down the mountainside, however, he caught sight of a buckskin cow pony grazing in scant grama grass, and the sight heartened him.

Shaking out the coils of his wet lass' rope once more, Sidlaw headed down the slope in quest of the pony. At a considerable distance beyond the buckskin he saw the horse he had ridden up from Smoketree, grazing near a clump of mesquites. The mustang was limping badly as a result of the accident in which the Phantom Sheriff had been hurled from the saddle the night before.

An expert cast and Sidlaw's rope settled about the buckskin's burr-clogged mane. It evidently had belonged to Rib Carson, for the dead smuggler's initials were on the saddlebags.

Sidlaw snubbed the rope to a pinon and caught the pony. Then, after repairing a frayed bridle rein, he rode back to the heap of rocks which marked the grave of the four dead outlaws.

"I need guns," mused Sidlaw, tying his horse to a rock, "so I got to turn grave robber an' like it."

It was gruesome business, scratching through the rubble to uncover corpses. He soon uncovered Pancho Pedro, wrapped in his filthy green serape. Rummaging under the woolen folds of the shroud, the Phantom Sheriff revealed the black rubber stocks of the Mexican's six-guns.

It was a common superstition among outlaws of the West that it was unlucky to wear a dead man's guns, hence the fact that Yuma and Shadmer had buried the corpses with their weapons in holsters.

But the Phantom Sheriff had no such fear as he removed Pancho Pedro's .45s from basket-woven holsters and inspected cylinders, triggers, and hammers.

Finding the Colts in good working order after he had blown dust from the bores, he stowed them in his own empty holsters. Then, because he could not be positive that his own belt ammunition was usable after his under-water dousing, the Phantom Sheriff transferred the cartridges from the Mexican's belts to his own.

"Shadmer must have decided to go against Curly Bardoo's warnin' an' return to Smoketree," reasoned Sidlaw as he scraped gravel back into the grave. "I kin attend to him later, especially since he thinks I'm dead. But Yuma—"

There was still a chance of overtaking Francisco Yuma, he knew. Authorities had been after the smuggling king for years, on both sides of the border, and Sidlaw was quick to see where his first duty lay. He tightened the buckskin's cinch and mounted. He was pleased to find that Carson's horse was well rested and responded to rein and spur.

In a few minutes he had picked up Yuma's trail and was heading for the skyline.

Topping Cartridge Peak, Sidlaw had a far-flung vista of the untamed Mexican wastelands. A faint smudge of dust following a twisting barranca on the south slope of the peak informed him as to the present whereabouts of Francisco Yuma and reassured him that he could ride safely down the mountain without fear of ambush.

"Reckon I'll take a short cut toward the end o' that canyon an' make up some o' the head start Yuma's got on me," decided the Phantom Sheriff, spurring the buckskin into a lope. "Travelin' on this rock won't cause any dust either. I cain't afford fer Yuma to git wise that he's bein' follered."

He regretted his lack of a long-range saddle rifle in the event that Francisco Yuma spotted him and the chase developed into a cross-country pursuit with the outcome hinging on their horses.

As it was, armed only with shortbarreled Colt .45s, any actual gunplay would have to occur within a hundred-foot radius to be effective.

Giving the buckskin its head, the waddy was soon galloping along a course parallel with the brushy barranca whose shady depths Yuma had chosen.

A sense of satisfaction suffused the waddy's being as he kept his eye on the drifting plume of dust marking the location of the homeward-bound smuggling king. Francisco Yuma, pockets filled with dinero from his contraband sales, was traveling slowly. After all, he had no cause to fear pursuit.

Few men ever traveled in these parched wastelands. And the remotest thing from Yuma's mind would be that the Phantom Sheriff, of all men, could be on his trail.

Sidlaw's reappearance would probably convince the Mexican outlaw that Sidlaw was, in truth, a phantom. Had he not seen the Wyoming cowboy hurled to his death in Rio Piedras gorge?

By the time it was necessary to rest the buckskin, Sidlaw had already passed the outlaw's position in the barranca. The exit from the dry wash was a half mile distant, and heavily brushed in with ocotilla, greasewood, and dwarf mesquites.

"I'll do my dangdest to take Yuma alive, I reckon," Sidlaw commented aloud, his eye dropping to the golden star on his dusty shirt front. "It'll be a good start on my job o' fillin' Freddie Clawson's boots fer ol' Buck, I reckon. Uncle Sam's boys will be plenty glad to question Francisco Yuma about his smugglin' activities these past few years."

The spirit of old Buck Clawson seemed to ride at Sidlaw's stirrup as he angled his bronc through the chaparral toward the barranca's mouth, out of which Yuma would soon be riding.

It was the dead sheriff's fight that Sidlaw was waging today, not his. The capture of Francisco Yuma had long been the fondest dream of Buck Clawson, equal even to the arrest of Gila Jack Shadmer and the destruction of the gambler's outlaw rule.

"I reckon Marie'd be plumb tickled, too, if I hauled Yuma to the gallows," mused the Phantom Sheriff. "It was one o' the jobs her brother would have tackled. I wonder—"

He broke off, embarrassed at his own trend of thought. What right had he, a drifting cowpoke, to believe that Marie Clawson could care one way or another about his activities, except as they were connected with his pledge to Freddie Clawson?

The mere fact that he was wearing the Phantom Sheriff's badge, the fact that destiny had cast him in the perilous role of a dead Texan, gave Sidlaw no valid reason for believing his actions could be of anything but casual interest to the daughter of the murdered sheriff of Malpais County.

His thoughts shifted abruptly as he found himself a hundred yards from the mouth of the low-walled canyon which formed a long, unbroken groove down the bleak slope of Cartridge Peak.

He was in the danger zone now. Already, Sidlaw could hear the hollow thud of steel-shod hoofs on stone, indicating that Francisco Yuma was nearing the open.

Dismounting, Sidlaw tied his buckskin to a saguaro stalk.

Then, unholstering his .45s, the lawman hurried across the sandy terrain until he came to a dense thicket of buck brush on the right flank of the barranca's entrance.

Even as Sidlaw knelt in the shadow of the brush, Francisco Yuma cantered out into the open, a dozen yards away.

Sunlight glinted off silver trappings on his bell-bottomed gaucho trousers and his saddle and martingale.

Yuma's pock-marked face was even more evil

by daylight than Sidlaw remembered it from the night before.

Completely unsuspicious of the presence of danger, Yuma was strumming on an imaginary guitar, while his palamino slowed to a trot as it reached level ground.

Holstering his left-hand gun, the Phantom Sheriff leaped out into the open.

"Hoist 'em, Yuma!"

Before the startled Mexican could drop hands to gun butts, Spook Sidlaw's left hand had seized the palamino's bit and jerked it to a halt.

Teeth flashing triumphantly, the Phantom Sheriff held the palamino at arm's length while he kept his blue-barreled .45 levelled at Francisco Yuma's gold-braided jacket.

"*Caramba*!" groaned the Mexican. "The Phantom Sheriff! You have returned from the dead!"

CHAPTER XV.

Overpowering surprise, not unmixed with superstitious terror, checked Francisco Yuma's instinctive movement to draw his guns for a shoot-out with the grinning young American who had leaped out of the buck brush to halt his pony.

"Thees—she ees eempossible!" muttered the smuggling king, slowly groping his arms aloft. "I saw you keeled, Senor Phantom. I must be dreaming."

The Phantom Sheriff reached up with a gun barrel and hooked the front sight under the curved stock of Francisco Yuma's nearest gun handle. Lifting the weapon out of its holster, Sidlaw flipped it deftly into the buck-brush clump.

"All right, Yuma. Light an' cool yore saddle a spell."

Trembling, the captured outlaw boss swung to the ground to confront the cool-voiced young buckaroo.

"Yuh ain't dreamin', Yuma. Yore nightmares from here on out will be inside o' prison bars."

Sidlaw jabbed his .45 into the Mexican's stomach, dropped his grip on the palamino's bridle and emptied Yuma's other holster.

Then he stepped back, eying his captive.

"Put yore hands behind yuh, Yuma," he

ordered. "I ain't got reg'lar handcuffs, but I kin hogtie yuh with a lariat, I reckon. Then we'll be takin' a pasear back to the Smoketree *juzgado*."

Yuma's shoe-button eyes had lost their fear and now regarded his captor sharply as he lowered his arms behind his body.

Only the fact that the Phantom Sheriff was on the alert for treachery saved him in the clipped heartbeat of time that followed.

Apparently slumped in total despair, Francisco Yuma suddenly pivoted on widespread legs, his right arm shooting outward like a catapulted rock.

Sunlight winked on a hard-flung *cuchillo* which Yuma had snatched from a hidden sheath behind him.

The knife made a whipping sound as it sped through space. But the Phantom Sheriff flung his body to one side and dropped into a squat.

Like a shaft of light the speeding blade hurtled past the spot occupied by the cowboy's body a split instant before and embedded itself in the green bole of a saguaro stalk a dozen feet away.

"I've heard you Mexies was expert at knife-throwin'," snapped Sidlaw as he got shakily to his feet. "But I didn't know yuh could git a sticker out o' leather an' flyin' through the air so quick. Yuh almost got me that time, Yuma."

The Mexican's upper lip curled away from broken yellow teeth in a leer that hid his baffled rage. He had played his final ace. He was aware that he was lucky Spook Sidlaw had not triggered a bullet into his chest in self-defense.

"I'm honin' to pack you back to Smoketree alive, Yuma," panted the lawman, warily approaching the Mexican. "So stick yore dew-claws in front o' yore belly an' put yore wrists together."

Yuma complied sullenly. Spook reached over to the palamino's saddle and unbuckled a coiled sisal-grass riata from the pommel. Holstering his gun, he deftly tied the Mexican's wrists together and tied them securely.

"Now, fork yore hoss," Sidlaw ordered, reaching for the bridle. "I reckon we'll head back to the Arizona side o' the border pronto."

Yuma gripped the dish-type Mexican saddle-horn clumsily with his bound-together hands, put boot to tapaderoed stirrup, and swung astride.

Gripping the palamino's bridle once more, Sidlaw headed back toward the cactus stalk where he had tied his own mount.

A sense of danger prompted the waddy to turn around. He was in time to see the smuggler pawing awkwardly at the butt of a Winchester which had escaped his attention because of a rolled-up poncho behind Yuma's cantle.

With a cry the Phantom Sheriff grabbed the barrel of the .30-30 even as Yuma struggled to lever a shell into the firing chamber.

The palamino, alarmed by a sudden struggle, swerved away. Yuma, clinging to the trigger guard of the Winchester, was pulled bodily out of the stirrups, landing with a crash that bore Sidlaw to the ground.

As they rolled over in a smudge of adobe dust, the frantic Mexican dropped his grip on the rifle to stab both hands toward the butt of one of Sidlaw's belt guns.

Frantically, the cowboy reached down to seize the muzzle of the gun, even as Yuma yanked it from the holster.

Hurling his entire weight against his wrist to divert the Mexican's aim, he heard Yuma pull the trigger, felt the searing heat as a bullet sped through the barrel of the .45 in his grasp.

But Sidlaw's straining muscles had forced the gun parallel to Yuma's chest.

The crash of the exploding .45 was so close to his head that Sidlaw winced, his ears filled with a whistling sound.

Smoke boiled in gray coils about their faces. Then, as Sidlaw wrenched the smoking gun out of Yuma's grasp to prevent him from firing again, the cowboy saw a thick trickle of crimson start oozing from the underside of Francisco Yuma's swarthy jaw.

"Reckon—that's finished—"

Death dulled the Mexican's snakelike eyes as

he sagged back, kicking the ground convulsively with clinking spurs.

Sidlaw stood up, fanning gunsmoke away from smarting eyes. He realized that Yuma's self-inflicted bullet had gone straight upward to lodge in his brain.

Sweat beaded Sidlaw's face as he realized how very nearly the daring Mexican had come to turning defeat into victory.

He stood in silence a moment, contemplating the twitching corpse of the Mexican who had been hunted so long on both sides of the border.

"I'm sorry Buck Clawson ain't here now," Sidlaw told the corpse gravely. "Smashin' yore smugglin' ring was one o' the sheriff's main ambitions."

Feeling suddenly weary, the Phantom Sheriff walked over to where Yuma's palamino waited dejectedly, as if sensing the fact that it would not feel its master's quirt and rowel again.

With a supreme effort, Sidlaw raised the Mexican's inert bulk to the saddle and tied him on at stirrups and at the saddlehorn.

Then Sidlaw led the palamino over to where his own buckskin waited patiently by the giant cactus. He mounted, dallied the Mexican's hackamore about his own saddlehorn and headed north.

Two hours later, the Phantom Sheriff, leading the palamino with its grisly burden, once more passed a cairn of rocks which marked the international boundary.

Reaching the flat country of Whispering Desert, he turned east along the Bisbee stage-coach road over the Dragoon Range, heading for Smoketree.

He passed no riders or wagons on the ten-mile trip along the stage road, and for that he was thankful. He did not want his return to Smoketree advertised just yet.

Approaching the little cow-town through the thick cactus forest, he entered Smoketree once more during the siesta hour.

"Seems queer that this time yesterday I was ridin' into this burg fer the first time," he mused absently. "Since then my whole life's changed. I'm wearin' the Phantom Sheriff's badge. An' I got a whole lot o' work cut out for me before I kin return that badge to Marie Clawson."

Unconsciously he let his eyes roam over to Mescal Hill, overlooking the town. Gleaming white in the sunlight, midway up the slope, was the little cottage where Sheriff Buck Clawson had died.

Several buckboard wagons were hitched to the front rail. Friends, no doubt, who had heard of the sheriff's death and had come to pay their respects and comfort Marie.

Then, as Sidlaw slanted his horses toward the Mexican quarter of town, he caught sight of a

126

crowd of bareheaded people standing inside a fenced-off enclosure farther to the eastward.

Sunlight glinted off ordered rows of tombstones. Flowers on two fresh mounds gave off a spot of varied color against the tawny background of the cemetery.

"Funeral services for the sheriff an' his son, Freddie, I reckon," surmised the waddy, a pang of sorrow clutching his heart. "Reckon this is a mighty blue hour fer pore little Marie—an' this bein' her nineteenth birthday, too."

He reined up in the yard back of Doc Frazer's house on the main street, glad that no one had seen his arrival in Smoketree with Francisco Yuma's corpse in tow.

Tying the palamino and the buckskin to Frazer's back fence, the Phantom Sheriff untied Francisco Yuma's body and carried it into the coroner's back room which served as a morgue.

He stretched the stiffening corpse on a stone slab where only the day before they had laid the body of Freddie Clawson.

After stabling the horses in Frazer's barn, Sidlaw headed for the main street, finding it deserted during the siesta period. He entered Willie Wong's All-American Restaurant and ordered a huge meal to satisfy the gnawing pangs of hunger which racked his body.

CHAPTER XVI.

Old Doc Frazer, accompanied by three sober-faced hombres who looked extremely ill at ease in the store clothes they had donned for the Clawson funeral in place of their customary chaps and steeple-peaked Stetsons, made his way up the front steps of the coroner's office and went inside.

Resting on a cot in the front office was a lanky waddy in red-checkered shirt, chocolate-brown chaps, and scuffed kangaroo leather cow boots.

Thinking at first that this was some cowpoke in town on an errand requiring a doctor, Frazer looked again and recognized the waddy as Spook Sidlaw.

"Talk o' the devil an' find him restin' his bones in my own office!" cried the grizzled old coroner of Malpais County, rushing forward to extend a hand in greeting. "I'm shore relieved to see yuh, son. When you left last night, honin' fer a showdown with Gila Jack Shadmer, I knowed I couldn't stop yuh. But I was plumb worried."

Sidlaw grinned. He had had a couple of hours' sleep following his meal at Willie Wong's Chinese cafe, and the rest had restored the sparkle to his agate-brown eyes and erased the harsh lines of fatigue which had stamped his bronzed countenance.

"That seems like a year ago, doc, since I left you up at Clawson's place," chuckled the Phantom Sheriff. "An' it makes me feel sheepish to have to admit that I crossed horns with Gila Jack an' come off second best. But I tallied Francisco Yuma, the smuggler. Yuh'll find his carcass in yore undertakin' parlor out back, doc."

Frazer gasped with astonishment.

"Kilt Yuma, huh? Buck Clawson would be tickled pink to know that smugglin' skunk has been—"

Frazer broke off, sorrow erasing the grin on his face at Sidlaw's news. He waved his three companions into chairs and seated himself on the couch alongside the man from Wyoming.

"We jest come from boothill," stated the cowtown doctor. "Buried the remains o' the sheriff an' young Freddie, one on either side o' Mrs. Clawson's grave. Anyways, as the preacher p'inted out, the Clawson family's reunited ag'in, just like all three of 'em would 'a' liked."

There was an awkward silence, during which Spook Sidlaw looked at the three strangers quizzically. He noticed that they failed to return his gaze, being intent on rolling wheat-straw-paper cigarettes.

"Oh—excuse me fer not introducin' my amigos hyar, Spook," apologized Frazer, observing the line of Sidlaw's scrutiny. "As a matter o' fact, they been champin' at the bit, wantin' to meet yuh. Yuh see, they're Buck Clawson's three depities."

Sidlaw stiffened, his eyes blazing as he looked over the trio. Frazer had informed him at supper yesterday that all of Buck Clawson's staff of deputies had turned in their badges the moment they learned that their chief had been ambushed.

"I know what you're thinkin'—that these depities got yaller streaks down their backs," hastened Doc Frazer. "But that's changed, Spook, since they heard you was wearin' the Phantom Sheriff's star an' aimin' to make Smoketree a decent town fer folks to live in."

The white-haired old medico got to his feet and proceeded to introduce each of the three men in turn:

"This long drink o' water is Slats Waterbury, jailer at our calaboose, Spook."

Long, lanky Slats Waterbury shuffled forward to shake hands. In spite of the distrust Sidlaw had built up for the three men he had ticketed for cowards, the Phantom Sheriff found himself warming to the trio.

"This chunky, pot-bellied old coot is Dick Cordell," continued Frazer. "He's packed a star fer forty year."

Pudgy, apple-cheeked Dick Cordell proudly thumbed back the lapel of his store suit to reveal a deputy sheriff's star that was tarnished by time.

"I'm right ashamed o' myself fer gittin' skittery an' handin' in my badge yestiddy," admitted Cordell over a handshake, "but I'll more'n make up for that, workin' fer you, Mr. Sidlaw—if yuh'll let me work for yuh."

The doctor presented a stripling younker with new fuzz on his chin next, introducing him as Sammy Duncan and informing Sidlaw that Duncan's father had sheriffed Malpais County before Buck Clawson hit the country.

Young Duncan, hardly out of his teens, shook hands gravely.

"Don't blame us too harsh fer quittin' yesterday, boss," pleaded the kid earnestly. "But Gila Jack Shadmer's been rowelin' this town so long— well, when we found out Buck wasn't goin' to be leadin' us any more, it seemed like plain suicide to go on tryin' to be law fellers in this skunk's nest. But it made us plumb ashamed o' ourselves when we heard you, a total stranger, was not afraid to be the new law o' Smoketree. So—"

The Phantom Sheriff turned to face Doc Frazer, his expression registering bewilderment.

"I . . . I didn't know I had any real official authority here in town, doc," he faltered. "I promised Freddie Clawson I'd tally Gila Jack Shadmer fer him, an' after I met Marie, I . . . I sort o' wanted to revenge her father's death. But I was figgerin' on doin' it solo, a lonewolf job."

The veteran medico sucked on his corncob pipe noisily to hide his pent-up emotions.

"Smoketree's sort o'—well, you're sort o' elected to fill Buck's shoes until we kin elect yuh legal, Spook," husked the coroner. "Smoketree needs a salty younker like you to take the reins. Some feller with guts an' the ability to sling a six-shooter. Why, last night if this town could 'a' laid hands on Shadmer—"

The Phantom Sheriff waved him off, remembering Curly Bardoo's description of the near riot which the townspeople had staged at the Lucky Dollars Saloon under Doc Frazer's peppery guidance.

"I know all about that, doc, an' I'm honored that yuh feel this way about it. But I think Marie Clawson ought to be consulted."

"Meanin' what, Mr. Sidlaw?" asked Slats Waterbury.

"Waal, this badge I'm totin' was her brother's. Her father was the sheriff whose place yuh want me to take. An' I admit I'm kind o' worryin' about how Marie's goin' to feel toward me, once her grief wears off an' she can think things over."

"I don't git yuh, Spook," protested Doc Frazer.

"Mebbe Marie might git to hatin' me fer indirectly causin' her brother's death. I wouldn't blame her if—"

A shadow fell across the door and a voice broke into their discussion:

"You needn't worry about that, Spook."

The four men spun about to face Marie Clawson, her cowgirl costume replaced by the simple black dress she had donned for the funeral.

"I'm so glad to . . . to see nothing happened to you last night," she said, extending her hand as she came forward. "And I want you to know I understand perfectly—about you and Freddie. I reckon Freddie would be proud to know you are wearing his star."

Sidlaw was conscious of a warm rush of red to his face as he took her hand. Frazer noted that the cowboy held it a trifle longer than necessary, and he grinned behind the pipe smoke.

"That . . . that's fine, Miss Marie," Sidlaw said. "I shore thank yuh. I reckon it'll be a help to me in tamin' this burg, knowin' you're backin' my play this way."

Sammy Duncan, who had been standing near the door, turned suddenly and cried out in a low voice:

"Sidlaw! Doc! Thar goes Gila Jack Shadmer!"

The Phantom Sheriff stiffened, dropping rope-calloused hands to the stocks of his guns as he brushed past Marie and went to the doorway.

He was in time to see the familiar black-coated figure of Gila Jack Shadmer entering the Lucky Dollars Saloon, accompanied by several cowpunchers who had just left their horses at the saloon's hitch bar.

"Shadmer had the nerve to come back to town after Curly Bardoo warned him—"

Sidlaw broke off, realizing that Shadmer believed him to be dead, down in Rio Piedras Canyon.

"Them buckaroos with him are some o' his Lazy Diamond crew, Spook!" Sammy Duncan told him. "The frog-built hombre was Slag Rubiez, his foreman. They're up to some devilment, I'll bet yuh."

Spook Sidlaw hitched his gun belts mechanically. His lips were compressed in grim determination as he faced his deputies.

As yet, he had no positive proof that they were the breed to back his play. Now would be as good a time as any to test their mettle and determine whether or not they meant their war talk of a few moments past.

"Boys, we got enough on Shadmer to hang him. What're we waitin' for?"

Doc Frazer's heart pounded with excitement as he watched the reaction of the three deputies. Of one accord they shucked their confining coats so as to get at their six-guns in a hurry if the occasion arose. Like war horses hearing a bugle, the deputies adjusted their Colt harness impatiently.

"Yeah—what're we waitin' fer?" demanded

Slats Waterbury, tucking a quid of tobacco in one toothless cheek. "Let's go haul Shadmer out o' his den!"

Marie Clawson rushed forward to catch the Phantom Sheriff's arm as he turned to go.

"Can't . . . can't you wait until after those Lazy Diamond men have left?" she pleaded. "You'd be committing suicide to try and arrest Gila Jack when he's got all his men around him, Spook. Please don't go!"

Sidlaw gently loosened her grip from his sleeve and glanced across at the coroner.

"Have a slab cleared off fer Shadmer's carcass, doc," ordered the new law of Smoketree. "We'll either bring Shadmer here, or clap him in the jailhouse yonder."

His expression softened as he saw the fear in Marie Clawson's eyes.

"Don't worry," he said softly, "I'm jest tryin' to find out if these depities o' yore dad's wear their guns fer decorative purposes. Besides, I can't risk Gila Jack Shadmer leavin' town."

Doc Frazer slid a fatherly arm about the girl's waist as the four lawmen trailed their spurs across the board sidewalk and headed for the Lucky Dollars Saloon, bent on a showdown that was long overdue.

CHAPTER XVII.

Whiskey fumes and tobacco smoke clogged the atmosphere of the big Lucky Dollars barroom as the Phantom Sheriff slammed open one of the green-slatted doors and stalked inside.

Behind him came Waterbury, Duncan and Cordell, thumbs hooked in cartridge belts, eyes scanning the row of drinkers at the bar, roving over the gamblers busy at baize-covered tables.

A hush descended over the saloon as its inmates recognized the four entrants as keepers of the law and order. Eyes bulged as they saw the gleaming gold star on Sidlaw's shirt. Word had spread in Smoketree, since the rebellion of the night before on the part of the townspeople, regarding the arrival of the famous Phantom Sheriff.

Sidlaw's narrowed eyes shuttled over the barroom, finding no trace of Gila Jack Shadmer's gigantic form.

A gagged sound came from the bar, and Sidlaw recognized Curly Bardoo, the bartender who had ridden out to the smugglers' meeting on Cartridge Peak the night before to warn his boss not to return to Smoketree until things had cooled down.

Now Bardoo was staring at the Phantom Sheriff

with hands shaking as if from ague. Had he not witnessed the certain destruction of this cold-eyed young waddy earlier that day?

"Gila Jack around?" demanded the Phantom Sheriff, striding over to where the pasty-faced bartender was staring at him in a paralysis of horror and disbelief.

"I . . . I reckon so. Only he left . . . left orders not to be disturbed fer nothin'. Him an' his *segundo*, Slag Rubiez, an' some o' his ranch hands are—"

Sidlaw headed for the door marked "Private," which he knew was Shadmer's office.

"That's all I wanted to know, Bardoo," clipped Sidlaw, his grim-faced trio of deputies at his heels. "Come on, pards."

Fifty pairs of eyes followed the four lawmen as they reached the door of Shadmer's private office. There was a nervous shifting of feet and chairs to break the deathly silence that had jelled the room.

Drawing a six-gun, the Phantom Sheriff reached down to twist the doorknob—and found it locked.

With one accord, Sidlaw and beefy-shouldered Dick Cordell drew back, then lunged at the door with terrific force.

Crash! Steel jangled and wood panels splintered as the lock gave way and the door slammed inward on protesting hinges.

In a brief glance the Sheriff took in the council scene inside Shadmer's office.

The boss outlaw himself was in the act of lighting a kerosene lamp hanging from a ceiling beam. At his elbow was a whiskery-jawed half-breed whom Duncan had identified as Slag Rubiez, foreman of Shadmer's huge Lazy Diamond spread, over in the Dragoon foothills.

Four other cowhands, tight-lipped and shifty-eyed, were in the act of drawing up chairs at a table preparatory to opening a bottle of Scotch.

"Lift 'em high, everybody!"

Sidlaw's steely voice froze Gila Jack Shadmer in a posture of surprise and bewilderment.

The Phantom Sheriff had counted on the unexpectedness of their entry, plus Shadmer's amazement at finding him supposedly returned from the dead, to give his deputies time to slip inside the room and get the drop on the Lazy Diamond hands.

Slag Rubiez made a hitching motion at his guns, then thought better of it as he found Sammy Duncan's Colt trained at his belly. The other cowhands merely stared in blank amazement.

Gila Jack Shadmer stood with jaw agape and eyes bulging in confusion as he saw the Phantom Sheriff edge in closer, gun barrels weaving over the group.

"What's—the idea, hombre?" Shadmer gasped

at last, licking his drooping lips. "Whar'd you git the authority to come bustin' in here like this—you an' Buck's tinhorn depities—"

The Phantom Sheriff's voice came like the tolling of a bell, sinister as a judge intoning a death sentence:

"We've come fer *you,* Gila Jack. After what happened on Cartridge Peak last night, you'd be silly to ask me why I'm takin' you under arrest."

Gila Jack Shadmer was no coward. A coward could not have arisen to his position of unchallenged power in Malpais County. In the few seconds that Spook Sidlaw had been speaking, Shadmer had overcome his dismay and surprise.

"Yuh . . yuh got a warrant?"

Sidlaw scowled angrily and clicked his .45 hammers.

"Throw up yore hands, Shadmer, or you'll be stretched out on Frazer's slab alongside o' yore amigo, Francisco Yuma. Reach!"

At the news of Yuma's death, Shadmer lost his composure. His arms lifted jerkily toward the ceiling.

"Don't prod him, boys," the outlaw warned his men. "Reckon he means business!"

Shadmer's words of surrender were only the prelude to pandemonium.

Lifting a knee in a swift, unseen motion under

the table, the towering gambler sent the table over on its side amid a flying confusion of liquor bottles, playing cards, and papers.

Dropping to a quick squat behind the upset table even as the Phantom Sheriff's guns bucked and blazed in his grasp, Gila Jack Shadmer snaked his own .45s from leather.

His first shot smashed the kerosene lamp overhead, plunging the room in semi-darkness.

Spook Sidlaw, who had received his baptism of bullets in more than one shoot-out up in Wyoming, had the savvy to dive for a shadow-blotted corner even as Shadmer opened fire, shooting through the pine top of the overturned table.

With a hoarse oath, Slag Rubiez danced aside and got his own .45s to blazing. Dimly, Spook Sidlaw heard Dick Cordell yelp with agony as churning bullets slammed into his paunchy belly, driving him to the floor before he could fire a shot.

Two waddies from the Lazy Diamond lunged at Sidlaw. A hail of slugs from fast-shooting Sammy Duncan dropped one of them bullet-riddled over a chair, while Sidlaw's thundering Colts sent slugs ripping into the skull of the second.

Taking advantage of the thick pall of gunpowder fumes which hung in bouncing milky layers throughout the room, Gila Jack Shadmer leaped for a side window overlooking an alley.

As he leaped for a getaway, Shadmer flung an arm about the wiry body of one of his cowhands, dragging him along toward the window even as Slats Waterbury and the Phantom Sheriff threw down their Colts in short, chopping motions at the escaping gambler.

Their bullets, intended for Shadmer, tunneled into the body of the cowhand whom the ruthless outlaw had seized for a living shield.

A back door slammed open, and out of the tail of his eyes the Phantom Sheriff saw the half-breed *segundo*, Slag Rubiez, make good his bolt for freedom.

The fourth remaining cowhand lifted a chair and flung it hard at Sammy Duncan. It shattered in a flurry of wooden fragments square in Duncan's face, dazing him.

Then the Lazy Diamond gun-hawk whipped Colts from leather and levelled them at Duncan as the stunned deputy sagged to his knees, fighting to keep his senses.

Gila Jack Shadmer, dropping the crimson-soaked body of his shielding cowhand, dived head and shoulders through the glass pane of the window to vanish outdoors.

Leaping after him, the Phantom Sheriff was forced to pause long enough to trigger a slug into the head of the cowboy who was in the act of gunning down Sammy Duncan.

The delay was disastrous. Even as the Phantom

Sheriff sprang to the window and stuck his head through the jagged glass, he caught sight of Gila Jack Shadmer and his foreman vaulting the low adobe wall that shut off the saloon's private livery stable and corral.

Frantically, Sidlaw drew a bead for a long shot at Shadmer, then groaned as his firing pin dropped on a dead cartridge with a mocking click. Before he could reload, Shadmer and Rubiez had disappeared.

Sick at heart, the Phantom Sheriff turned back to face the shambles in Shadmer's smoky office. It was not a pretty scene.

Dick Cordell lay slumped in death by the door jamb. Three of the Lazy Diamond hands were sprawled grotesquely amid the wreckage of table and chairs, their blood blending with the spilled puddles of whiskey on the floor.

Sammy Duncan's face was torn and gore-smeared as a result of the chair striking him. Slats Waterbury was squeezing a bullet-gashed forearm, crimson worming through his fingers as he bit his lips to keep from moaning.

Fifty seconds had elapsed since they had battered their way into the private office of Gila Jack Shadmer. Death had already claimed four victims in that ghastly interval of time, but the man they had come to arrest was galloping out of town by now.

Curly Bardoo, the bartender, appeared in the

doorway, clutching a sawed-off shotgun. He retreated as Spook Sidlaw crossed the room and slammed the door in his face to keep out the curious jam of spectators who had heard the shooting.

"Anyhow, the meanest hombre on Shadmer's crew is goin' to croak," panted Slats Waterbury, pointing at the writhing body of the Lazy Diamond hand whom Shadmer had carried along with him to the window as a living shield against law bullets.

"Who is he, Waterbury?" questioned Sidlaw, busy reloading his six-guns.

"Gus Madson, chief. Hoss wrangler on the Lazy Diamond spread. He's kilt a dozen men, not countin' Mexies or Injuns, to my knowledge. Even served a stretch over in Yuma fer train robbery."

The Phantom Sheriff squatted down beside the badly wounded ex-convict, Gus Madson. He realized that the Lazy Diamond horse wrangler would pay for his life as a result of Shadmer's action in seizing him for a shield.

"Anyhow, Madson," Sidlaw told the ashen-faced killer, "afore yuh cross the Big Divide yuh kin have one comfortin' thought. Gila Jack Shadmer's goin' to end up in boothill if it's the last thing I ever do."

A shudder of rage and pain shook Gus Madson's frame.

"The dirty polecat . . . grabbed me . . . made me take the slugs yuh intended fer him," panted the dying wrangler. "But . . . I reckon I'll git even . . . with Shadmer. Listen close, busky. I'll tell yuh somethin' . . . plumb interestin'!"

Sidlaw frowned, wondering what Madson was driving at. The dying horse wrangler heaved a deep breath, spat crimson bubbles off his lips, and continued in a voice that shook with a fierce desire for revenge against the man who had caused his doom:

"The reason . . . we was meetin' with Shadmer jest now . . . was to discuss . . . plans to . . . rustle a thousand head o' beef . . . tomorrow," were Madson's startling words. "A special cow train o' the Arizona and Western Railway . . . will be comin' through Whisperin' Desert—"

Sammy Duncan squatted down beside the Phantom Sheriff, laying a hand on the waddy's knee.

"Peel yore ears to this, boss," whispered Duncan. "Madson's pizen sore, an' he's goin' to spill some o' Jack Shadmer's secret info. This ought to be worth listenin' to—"

Madson choked, then went on in a rapidly fading voice:

"This hyar cow train is due . . . at Gunbore Tunnel . . . around three o'clock. Shadmer an' us Lazy Diamond hands . . . was goin' to hide . . . at the Antelope Ridge loadin' pens. We was goin'

144

to flag the train . . . hogtie the crew . . . an' force the engineer to run us on through the Dragoons."

"Yeah—go on, Madson," urged the Phantom Sheriff.

"Out in the middle o' Whisperin' Desert . . . we was aimin' to stop the train ag'in, miles from nowhar . . . unseal the car doors . . . an' haze the cattle up into Lazy Diamond range," whispered Madson. "We was goin' to . . . blot their brands . . . sell 'em south o' the border in a few weeks—"

The Phantom Sheriff felt his neck prickle with excitement as he considered the import of Madson's amazing disclosure.

Dying, the angry horse wrangler was tipping them off to one of the cleverest and most daring schemes for wholesale cattle thievery that the cowboy had ever listened to.

"Hide near that side track . . . at Antelope Ridge . . . with a posse," gurgled Madson faintly. "Yuh'll be able . . . to nab Gila Jack . . . in the act. I hope . . . he finds out I was the one . . . to tip yuh off!"

Sidlaw put a hand on Madson's red-stained shoulder.

"Thanks, Madson," he said softly. "Don't worry—we'll be on hand to put a kibosh on Shadmer's rustlin' job tomorrow. We—"

He broke off as he realized he was talking to a dead man.

"You stay here till I send the coroner over to

take charge o' these bodies, Sammy," the sheriff said crisply.

Leaving by the back door so as not to have to run the gantlet of the excited throng in the barroom, the Phantom Sheriff returned to Doc Frazer's place.

"Got some business fer yuh, doc," he said bluntly, jerking a thumb toward the Lucky Dollars Saloon. "But, sorry to say, Gila Jack's ain't among the carcasses."

He turned to face Marie Clawson, who had jumped up from a sofa to greet him, relief plainly written on her face.

"Miss Marie," he said, grinning boyishly, "doc tells me you used to be almost a reg'lar depity sheriff fer yore dad. I wonder if you know all the ranchers in Malpais County—them that don't cotton to Gila Jack Shadmer, I mean?"

"Reckon I do, Spook. I've lived here ten years."

"O.K. Listen, Marie. I need somebody to ride around to these ranches, come daylight tomorrow. I got a big job ahead of me, an' I'll need a posse—every honest rider we kin rake together. You reckon you could help round 'em up for me?"

She flashed even white teeth in a smile and reached out to shake his hand with slim fingers.

"You bet! Be glad to help—pardner!" she said.

CHAPTER XVIII.

The Arizona sun blazed down on a sweating posse of Malpais County ranchmen and gun-hung residents of Smoketree, gathered here at the west end of Gunbore Tunnel.

The rusty tracks of the little-used Arizona & Western Railway emerged from the tunnel to stretch off into the heat-shimmering distance, flanking the Dragoon range.

Marie Clawson had had a hand in rounding up most of the outlying ranchers in the posse. Eager to help end the lead-law rule which Gila Jack Shadmer had forced upon Malpais County for years past, the ranchmen had flocked to the Phantom Sheriff's call. Now, grim and deadly earnest, they waited intently for the young lawman to outline his plans.

"It's three miles to that sidetrack at Antelope Springs whar Shadmer's rustlers are plannin' to flag the train," explained the Phantom Sheriff. "It wouldn't do to tackle 'em out on the open flats. They'd see us comin' an' scatter."

The Phantom Sheriff pointed to the mouth of the tunnel.

"I want twenty-five of you fellers to remain on this side o' Gunbore Tunnel," he said. "Yuh'll be in charge o' my deputy, Slats Waterbury, thar.

147

The rest of yuh will hide in the brush an' rocks at the east entrance o' the tunnel."

"An' what," drawled Ezra Blaine, one of the biggest range holders in the group of ranchmen, "will you be doin', son? You tryin' to take all the fun fer yoreself, an' leave us here?"

Sidlaw grinned and shook his head, eying his possemen.

"Here's the plan," he sketched briefly. "I'll ride alone down to Antelope Ridge loadin' yards. I'll keep myself hidden until the rustlers have stopped the train an' boarded it. Then I'll jump on an' when the train starts climbin' that grade on the other side o' the tunnel, I'll start settin' hand brakes on the cars.

"That'll force the train to come to a stop, an' if I figger it right, the train will stop inside o' Gunbore Tunnel. Get the idea, men? That'll be yore cue to come out o' hidin'—an' yuh'll have Gila Jack Shadmer an' his whole crew bottled up. We'll put a stop to his cow thievin' in one haul!"

After a few minutes more of discussion, to get details of the proposed wholesale capture firmly fixed in their minds, the group split into halves. Slats Waterbury's division remained at the exit of Gunbore Tunnel. The remaining two dozen riders, including Sammy Duncan and Doc Frazer, hid themselves in the thickets of brush and nests of boulders on the east end.

From the top of the ridge Spook Sidlaw got

a clear view of the valley beyond, with the Antelope Ridge loading pens clearly visible.

Keeping to heavy brush, so as not to be spotted by Shadmer's rustler outfit, which he believed was hidden among the adobe sheds at the sidetracks, the Phantom Sheriff headed into the valley.

He kept under the rim of a long barranca, emerging from the wash a half-hour later to find himself opposite and a quarter mile north of the weather-beaten sheds and corral fences of the Antelope Ridge siding.

Uncasing a pair of binoculars which hung from his saddlehorn, Sidlaw scanned the loading pens with the powerful lenses. He caught sight of men moving among the board-roofed sheds.

"Shadmer an' his rustlers are holin' up already," he cried excitedly, casing the glasses. "I reckon I'll have to watch my step if I git close to the tracks by the time they flag the train."

He swung his eyes to the eastward. Faintly visible on the horizon miles away he could see a crawling object at the vanishing point of the railroad tracks, trailing a feather of dark smoke along the sky. The cow train was already in sight!

He was riding the buckskin he had brought from Cartridge Peak two nights before. Realizing the impossibility of spanning the intervening ground to the railroad track on horseback, without being spotted by Shadmer's bunch, Sidlaw dismounted and hobbled the buckskin.

Then he headed off through the cactus and mesquites, working his way stealthily toward the tracks.

The whistle of the approaching cattle train wafted to his ears by the time he had crawled within a dozen feet of the roadbed, his body hidden in dense thickets of Russian thistles immediately opposite the cattle-loading sheds.

There was an excited hum of men's voices from the corrals, and as Sidlaw lay prostrate he caught the brittle voice of Gila Jack Shadmer issuing final orders:

"Now, yuh all know what yore jobs are, boys. Most o' the brakemen will be ridin' in the caboose, I reckon. Convers, yuh're responsible fer seein' that the train crew is herded into that adobe shack yonder an' locked up. If any of 'em draw a hogleg, shoot—but I don't think the brakies will be packin' artillery."

"We git yuh, boss."

"Rubiez an' me will jump the engine as soon as we've flagged her to a stop, an' take care o' the hoghead an' fireman. We'll yank the whistle cord when we're ready to hightail. If any o' you fellers ain't aboard the caboose, shoot off a hogleg."

"We're all set, boss."

"O.K., then. She's gettin' close, so keep under

cover—an' keep quiet, until I give the signal."

Rails hummed as the oncoming cow train hurtled at a fifty-mile clip down the tracks, gaining speed for the long mountain grade looming ahead.

Then Spook Sidlaw caught sight of Gila Jack Shadmer emerging from a loading chute, waving his black sombrero as he stood in the middle of the tracks.

A raucous whistle came from the train, followed by a screech of brake shoes on steel wheels.

From his hiding place in the thistles, Sidlaw could watch Shadmer standing his ground beside the loading pens, flagging down the train with cool indifference.

Belching black smoke and jetting clouds of noisy steam, the Arizona & Western cattle train grated to a clanging halt, its cowcatcher a few feet from where Shadmer stood.

Slag Rubiez made his appearance alongside the fireman's side of the cab as Shadmer hurried past the huge drive wheels.

The six-gun in Rubiez's hand roared and the overall-clad fireman who had leaped to the cab door pitched out on the right of way, chest drilled by a bullet.

Even as the startled engineer turned from his brake lever, Gila Jack Shadmer swarmed up the iron steps to cover the hoghead with a cocked .45.

"Drop that wrench, hombre!" Sidlaw heard the outlaw's order. "We're takin' over this train, an' you'll obey orders or git the same dose o' lead pizen yore fireman jest got!"

Farther down the tracks, gun-toting outlaws came out of hiding to commandeer the freight conductor and seven gaping brakemen who had jumped out of the caboose to investigate the unscheduled stop at Antelope Ridge siding.

Bristling guns forced the train crew to march toward an adobe shed. A door slammed and a bolt was thrown in place. From the caboose end of the train came a hoarse yell from a rustler:

"Hull crew's locked up, Jack. Let's go!"

Cattle bawled deafeningly in the red stock cars which formed the train. Spook Sidlaw saw the white-faced engineer, quailing before the menace of levelled guns, release his air brakes and pull the throttle bar.

Rustlers at the back end of the train were swinging aboard the caboose as the locomotive snorted a volcano of black smoke. The rattle of couplers and grind of drive wheels on rails drowned the nervous bawling of the beef steers confined in the cars.

Sidlaw caught a glimpse of Shadmer and Rubiez standing in the locomotive cab as the puffing engine rolled past the spot where the sheriff lay in hiding. Both outlaws were intent on the engineer.

Bracing himself for action, the Phantom Sheriff rose out of the weeds and ran alongside the tracks. The car immediately behind the locomotive was a flatcar partially loaded with railroad ties, and Sidlaw's fingers closed about a ladder rail at the front end.

Running a few steps as the train gathered speed, Sidlaw swung up on the iron step and scrambled onto the flatcar, crawling at once behind a tier of fresh-sawed railroad ties.

"Made it without bein' seen, I reckon," he panted, tugging at the chin strap of his Stetson. "Startin' from a dead stop thisaway, that engineer ain't goin' to git much speed up when he hits the grade this side o' Gunbore Tunnel, so I reckon my scheme'll work *bueno*."

The Arizona landscape swam past to a slowly increasing *clickety-click* of wheels over rail joints. Sidlaw, his back to the tier of railway ties, hooked elbows about his legs and bent his face down against the beat of the wind which was carrying smoke and cinders down upon the flatcar.

For a moment the whipping black smoke lifted, and as Sidlaw glanced up, his heart froze with horror.

Leaping from the rear of the locomotive tender to the flatcar came Slag Rubiez, the Lazy Diamond *segundo*.

A six-gun was in the foreman's hand, and, even

153

as his boots landed with a thud upon the plank floor of the flatcar, Rubiez swung the .45 to cover Spook Sidlaw.

Before the Phantom Sheriff could stab a hand to his own guns, Rubiez pulled the trigger.

CHAPTER XIX.

A lurch of the jouncing cattle train threw the Lazy Diamond foreman off balance, at the instant that a forked tongue of flame spat from the bore of his Colt.

The slug thudded into the cedar railroad ties at the Phantom Sheriff's back, even as Sidlaw bounced to his feet and lunged at Rubiez, left arm swatting at the foreman's gun barrel. One shot from Rubiez, if it reached the ears of Gila Jack Shadmer in the locomotive cab up in front, might pass unnoticed in the din of sound. But if a gun battle followed, Spook Sidlaw knew it would bring discovery, and ruin his chances of making a wholesale capture of Shadmer's rustler crew.

Driving a knuckle-bunched fist into Rubiez's hairy jaw, Sidlaw knocked the outlaw straw boss back against the rusty iron wheel of the flatcar's hand brake.

Rubiez, squalling oaths, landed on his back on the splintery floor of the flatcar, his head overhanging the coupling bar as Spook Sidlaw landed on his gun arm with both feet, forcing the rustler foreman to let go his smoking Colt.

Crying out fiercely, Rubiez fought with gorilla-like fury to throw off the waddy whose hands were seeking to clamp a viselike grip on his throat.

Bracing himself against the brake bar, Rubiez grappled with Sidlaw and the two came to their feet, fists slamming ribs, boot heels grating on the wooden floor.

With a snarl, Rubiez brought up a knee to crash it hard into the pit of Sidlaw's stomach. The maneuver broke the clinch, drove Sidlaw back, staggering, gagging for breath.

Before Rubiez could get his other gun out of leather for a pay-off shot at point-blank range, Sidlaw brought up a smoking uppercut that landed with a whiplike *smack* across the point of the *segundo*'s jaw.

Knocked backward by the terrific punch, Rubiez collapsed with wind-milling arms into the gulf of space between the locomotive's coal car and the front end of the flatcar.

Sidlaw paled with horror as he saw Rubiez drop backward down onto the rattling drawbar of the locomotive.

For an instant the bandit's body jackknifed over the big hose coupling of the air-brake system. Then, before the Phantom Sheriff could stoop to grab the doomed man, Slag Rubiez was snatched out of sight under the swimming blur of steel rails and cinder-clotted ties.

Sidlaw groped out a hand to seize the brake wheel for support, his stomach knotted with revulsion as he realized that Rubiez had gone to a gory death under the roaring wheels of the cattle cars. The foreman's body would be ground to hash meat by the time the caboose had passed over it.

"I just wonder," panted Sidlaw, wiping clammy moisture off his face with a red-checkered sleeve, "if Rubiez saw me git aboard an' climbed back over the coal pile to kill me, or if he was just on his way back to the caboose to take charge of his men."

But the locomotive thundered on, indicating that Gila Jack Shadmer still kept his post beside the engineer. Black smoke funneled from the locomotive's smokestacks, proof that the hoghead was having a difficult time climbing the mountain grade from his dead stop at the Antelope Ridge sidetrack.

"If them buskies in the caboose happen to spot Rubiez's carcass on the tracks, my scheme's done for," mused Sidlaw uneasily. "They'd signal Shadmer to stop the train an' investigate, an' I'd be discovered fer shore."

He waited several minutes, eyes glued to the rim of the locomotive tender, in case Gila Jack Shadmer came back. But nothing happened. The engine was churning its wheels over the rails, struggling to keep its speed as it labored up the grade toward Gunbore Tunnel.

Sidlaw waited until landmarks told him he was

within two hundred yards of the mouth of the tunnel where his possemen were hidden.

"With the train havin' all it kin do to keep rollin', I reckon it'll be easy to stop it," he decided, reaching for the brake wheel. "I reckon Gila Jack's due fer a bad surprise."

Bracing his feet, Sidlaw gave the wheel three turns before he felt the brake shoes begin to throw sparks from locked trucks.

That done, he hurried back down the flatcar, clinging to piles of railway ties for support, until he came to the rear-brake wheel. Soon the high-pitched shriek of locked wheels against rails told him that the locomotive was dragging the flatcar by main force.

Sidlaw gauged the distance to the first cattle car and leaped to the steel ladder running up its end. He clung to the ladder for a moment, peering forward to see if he were visible from Gila Jack Shadmer's position in the engine cab. But the intervening tender, with its water tanks and mountain of coal, hid him from view.

Smoke and hot cinders beat against his back, but offered him a protective screen as he climbed to the catwalk on the roof of the cattle car and set the brake wheel there.

The mouth of Gunbore Tunnel was only a hundred yards away now, and the train was slowing perceptibly under the drag of the braked wheels.

Spook Sidlaw knew that he was being watched by Sammy Duncan, Doc Frazer and the score of possemen hidden in the brush flanking the tunnel. They were in readiness to pounce on the rustlers in the caboose as soon as the train halted.

The locomotive snorted with renewed power as the engineer opened the throttle in an effort to offset the dragging wheels.

Running along the double-plank catwalk on the top of the cattle car, Sidlaw barely had time to set the rear-brake wheel and then fling himself on his stomach, before daylight was blotted out by the arched roof of Gunbore Tunnel, a scant three feet above him.

The screech of sliding wheels on the two cars, blended with the thunder of the locomotive, deafened Sidlaw. Smoke threatened to choke him, as it beat down from the soot-laden roof of Gunbore Tunnel.

Beyond the belching stack of the overloaded engine, the semicircular exit of Gunbore Tunnel was growing in size, a dot of blazing white against the jet blackness of the tunnel walls.

Up in the locomotive's cab, Gila Jack Shadmer leaped to the engineer's side, his foul oaths lashing the hoghead's ears.

"Stop settin' them air brakes, dang yuh, or I'll kill yuh!"

The bewildered engineer pointed at his open brake lever.

"*I* ain't puttin' on them brakes—I swear it!" he babbled frantically, jerking his throttle wide open. "It must be yore men back thar, settin' the hand brakes!"

Shadmer leaped to the cab window, peering out to see that the cattle train was going at a slower and slower pace as the rough, blasted walls of Gunbore Tunnel slid past in the darkness.

"Yore train's stoppin', I tell yuh. Keep it goin'!"

The engineer's face was a pasty mask of fright in the eerie, dancing light from the firebox door.

"I cain't help it. I cain't understand it. Must be some hotboxes slowin' us down, back thar somewhar. My steam pressure ain't dropped yet, so I know it ain't the engine's fault!"

The churning drive-wheels of the locomotive began spinning uselessly on the rails, as the weight of dragging cars overcame the power of the steam throttle.

Sparks flew from the drivers as the engineer opened a petcock to release sand from the boiler dome to the rails. But even the added friction afforded by the sand did not help.

Panting like an exhausted animal, the engine came to a halt, its cowcatcher not yet outside Gunbore Tunnel. Automatically the engineer reached up to shut the throttle, in order to halt the madly spinning drive-wheels.

Gila Jack Shadmer's gun barrels glinted in the

ruby light from the grate, as he swung them to cover the horrified engineer.

"Open that throttle, dang yuh! Git this train movin'!"

The engineer spread his hands in a gesture of despair.

"Won't do no good. I got to see if we got a hotbox—"

Crash! Shadmer's guns exploded harshly above the panting of the stalled locomotive.

His skull pierced by converging slugs, the engineer rolled to the steel floor of the cab and fell with his cheek against the firebox, the odor of scorching flesh rising to assail Gila Jack Shadmer's nostrils.

The rustler boss stepped to the cab window and looked out once more. Then his jaw sagged in dismay as he saw men bearing rifles and shotguns leap out of the brush flanking the mouth of Gunbore Tunnel and start walking down the track, their guns aimed at the doors and windows of the caboose where the Lazy Diamond cow-hands were riding.

The Lazy Diamond owner swore harshly, as realization of what was happening flooded his brain. "This is a trap. We been bottled up inside this damn tunnel!"

Swinging his gaze back toward the exit of the tunnel, Shadmer was appalled to see a row of grim-faced Smoketree citizens, led by Slats

161

Waterbury, grimly blocking the track, six-guns and rifles in readiness to shoot any outlaw attempting to escape the tunnel.

Shadmer knew his life would hinge on his action in the next few seconds, before Waterbury's men entered the tunnel to take charge of the stalled locomotive.

The gambler's knowledge of railroading was scant, but he had worked around cattle-loading tracks enough to know how to uncouple cars.

Leaping to the fireman's door of the engine cab, Shadmer swung to the ground and hurried along the tender to its rear end.

Ducking between the coal car and the flatcar loaded with ties, Shadmer tugged at a steel bar and released the couplers. Another lever disengaged the air-brake hose, and then Shadmer was running back to the cab.

Even as he rushed to the throttle and opened it as he had seen the slain engineer do, he heard Waterbury's shout ring down the tunnel:

"You, in the engine! Come out with yore hands up!"

Smoke puffed thunderously from the loco-motive as its wheels obeyed the drive of steam-jetted cylinders. Gaining speed, the engine of the cattle train, released of its load, drew away from the halted cars behind it.

Shadmer dropped behind the protection of the engineer's seat as the locomotive puffed out into the blazing sunshine, scattering Waterbury and his possemen who had sought to block the track.

A yelling hombre, whom Shadmer recognized as Willie Wong, proprietor of the All-American Cafe in Smoketree, caught the handrail of the cab door as the locomotive roared past like an unleashed iron giant.

For an instant the moon-faced Chinese stared at Shadmer's crouching figure, then brought up an old-fashioned Paterson model Colt and thumbed back the hammer.

Shadmer's six-gun spat flame and smoke, and the yellow-skinned Oriental flopped from sight. An instant later his body hit the right of way and rolled aside into the weeds.

CHAPTER XX.

Spook Sidlaw was bellying down on the catwalk atop the first cattle car, when he felt the train grate to a halt. From his vantage point he saw Slats Waterbury and his men leap from hiding and line up across the tracks, blocking escape from that end of the tunnel.

The young sheriff dared not stand up, even if the soot-grimy ceiling of Gunbore Tunnel had permitted, for he knew that Waterbury or one of the other possemen might shoot him for an outlaw.

A shot from the locomotive cab made Sidlaw drop flatter.

A minute after the single shot, the Phantom Sheriff saw the locomotive snort into life and start drawing away from the train proper. In an instant, Sidlaw realized that Gila Jack Shadmer had pulled a surprise move and was trying to escape in the locomotive, leaving his rustler crew to face the music.

With a yell, Sidlaw leaped down to the flatcar, raced to its front end and sprang to the ground.

Running at top speed, Sidlaw yelled a warning to the scattering posse members, even as he followed the rolling train out into the sunlight.

Slats Waterbury and his men held their fire as

they recognized their red-shirted leader and saw him make a flying leap and catch a foothold on the rear step of the locomotive tender.

The corpse of the murdered Chinaman rolled through the dust as Spook Sidlaw peered back at the rapidly-dwindling figures of his posse, and as they watched the fugitive locomotive thunder on up the grade.

Ties blurred past under Sidlaw's boot heels as he braced himself against the whipping wind and crawled up the steel ladder to the top of the coal car.

His Stetson tugged at its chin cord as the waddy crawled over the rim of the car and dropped down onto the pile of coal.

He crouched there a moment, watching the mountainside wheel past the speeding locomotive as it rocked around a curve of the Dragoon ridge. Tumbling clouds of black smoke beat against his face, smudging his nostrils, biting his throat.

The rusty old cattle-train engine was rocketing down a grade now at a mile-a-minute clip. Freed of its burden of cars, the engine was swaying perilously as it thundered on.

"Got to stop Shadmer afore he wrecks this an' kills us both."

Spook Sidlaw slid a .45 Colt from leather and started crawling up the heap of coal.

A moment later he peered over the top of the

coal bin, eyes slitted against the beating sparks from the engine's smokestack.

Gila Jack Shadmer was seated on the engineer's cushioned bench, peering backward along the track as if he expected pursuit. Huddled in the winking glow of the firebox was the corpse of the overall-clad engineer.

Knowing that the noise of wheels and exhaust would drown the sound of his scrambling down the crest of the coal pile, Spook Sidlaw got to his feet and waded ankle-deep through the coal, then skidded in a small avalanche to the floor of the tender.

Gila Jack immediately whirled around, hand dropping to a holstered Colt as he caught sight of Spook Sidlaw crouching between the twin water tanks of the tender. Spook's eyes glittered a warning over the levelled barrel of his six-gun.

"Shut off that throttle, Shadmer!" yelled the Phantom Sheriff above the din of the speeding locomotive. "Then get yore paws above yore ears, savvy?"

Shadmer braced himself against the engineer's window, figuring his chances of getting a gun into action from swivel holsters in the event that a lurch of the coal car threw Spook Sidlaw off balance for a fraction of a second.

The crouching sheriff divined Shadmer's intention and triggered a warning slug through the glass window at the outlaw's shoulder.

Splinters of flying glass sprayed against the rustler chief's face and made him jerk his hands off the low-slung butt of his Colt.

Without taking his eyes from Sidlaw's gun bores, Shadmer reached up an exploring hand, found the handle lever of the throttle bar, and closed it a few notches.

Instantly the engine slowed down, freed from the driving pressure of steam in its cylinders.

Swaying like a sailor on a stormy deck, Spook Sidlaw stepped warily forward into the cab proper. The body of the dead engineer rolled gruesomely with the jouncing of the floor. The hot blast of the firebox smote the sheriff's face as he lifted his voice to shout at the bayed outlaw standing before him:

"I said *close that throttle,* Shadmer. Then unbuckle yore gun harness an' toss 'em out the window, so yuh won't get tempted to git boogery."

Gila Jack Shadmer, for all his reputation as a ruthless bad man of the border, was game. But he realized that Sidlaw needed very little prodding to start shooting.

With a snarl, Shadmer shut off the throttle, reached down, and unbuckled first one cartridge belt, then the other. Next he stooped to untie the buckskin thongs which held his left-leg holster to his thigh. After that, with a sideward motion of his arms, he tossed guns, holsters and ammunition belts out the cab window.

Not until then did the Phantom Sheriff relax.

"Which one o' them gadgets sets the brakes?" the cowboy lawman demanded, glancing nervously at the mountainside that was zipping past outside. "We're goin' downgrade now, an' this ol' boiler will leave the rails if we don't slow up."

Shadmer reached for the shiny-brass handle which controlled the engine's air brakes. The engine, despite its closed throttle, was picking up speed as it coasted down the west slope of the ridge.

With a quick jerk of his hand, Shadmer set the air brakes, then released them suddenly.

The sudden clamp of steel shoes on wheels threw the Phantom Sheriff violently forward against the maze of pipes, dialed gauges and other machinery on the boiler head.

Instantly seizing his moment of advantage, Shadmer lunged from the seat cushion and locked an elbow around Sidlaw's head.

Hurling his weight against Sidlaw, the rustler boss threw his captive on his back against the steel-plated floor.

Stars flew in front of Sidlaw's eyes as the outlaw's hard fist smashed across his cheekbones.

Desperately trying to roll his body off his own gun, Spook felt Gila Jack Shadmer's knees jut forward to pin his arms against the floor plates.

For an instant Sidlaw stared up at Shadmer's

contorted face, painted a lurid scarlet by the dancing flames in the engine's grate.

He saw Shadmer snatch up a crescent wrench, poise it murderously. Then he jerked his head to one side, and heard the wrench clang harshly against the floor plates.

Powerless to use the gun in the hand pinned down by Shadmer's knee, the Phantom Sheriff reared to a sitting position, grabbing desperately at the steel wrench in Shadmer's fist.

With a grunting effort, Sidlaw broke the agonizing pressure of Shadmer's knee on his arm, though the move cost him possession of the six-gun he had been clutching.

He jumped to his feet, driving a haymaker at Shadmer's eye.

There was no time to go for his other gun. Sidlaw ducked frantically to escape Shadmer's charge, swiveling his shoulder out from under the downward drive of the outlaw's wrench.

Sidlaw lost his footing on the engineer's corpse, and both fighters reeled off balance, only to jump to their feet again, each man clinging to opposite ends of the crescent wrench while their free fists slugged each other with lightning-swift jabs.

Spook Sidlaw was on the defense, now. Shadmer knew that if he gave the cowboy lawman an instant's respite, Sidlaw would unholster his other Colt and finish the fight with a single bullet.

Bracing himself against a flesh-crushing hail of blows, Spook Sidlaw felt himself driven back against the fireman's seat box. A sidelong glance outside showed him a danger more certain than the fists and kicking boots of his opponent.

The speeding locomotive was approaching a sharp bend in the tracks, overlooking a long, cactus-dotted slope.

And the Phantom Sheriff, unfamiliar though he was with handling a train, realized that the engine would go off the rails if it were not slowed down in the next few seconds.

Ducking a smoking uppercut, he slapped an arm to his side and brought up his cocked .45 at last.

Shadmer jumped back, releasing his grip on the wrench and raising his arms in surrender.

"Slam that brake—Shadmer—quick—"

Blood leaked in triple threads from Shadmer's crushed lips. His eyes glared like a crazy man's through a disheveled mop of hair. He only stared, too punch-drunk to comprehend Sidlaw's frantic order.

And then, even as the Phantom Sheriff leaped for the brake lever himself, the locomotive hit the curve at breakneck speed.

The scream of protesting wheel flanges against loosening rails put an ache in the ears of the two battered men in the cab.

Then spikes tore loose from weather-worn ties,

and the runaway locomotive catapulted off the tracks to go rocketing down the mountainside, its cowcatcher plowing into the dirt as it hurtled madly down the slope, still erect on its own wheels.

CHAPTER XXI.

The six-gun was knocked from Sidlaw's hand as he was hurled violently against the boiler's array of gauges and petcocks.

He caught a brief glimpse of Gila Jack Shadmer, sprawling backward over the engineer's corpse as the careening locomotive sprawled its way at terrifying speed down the hillside.

Out the window, the Phantom Sheriff got a terrifying view of a deep, rock-walled canyon at the foot of the slope. The engine was still on its wheels by some miracle, the slant of the mountainside preventing it from tipping over on its side.

Doom was a matter of clock ticks away, and the Phantom Sheriff knew that his chance of escaping the smash-up of the engine was one against hundreds.

Then the hurtling engine hit a curving dune of drifted sand. Only the fact that he struck the limp corpse of the engineer underfoot kept Spook Sidlaw's head from being cracked open like a ripe melon as he was thrown off his feet by the impact.

Sidlaw crawled toward the fireman's side of the cab as he felt the engine beginning to topple over on its side.

Like a frog hopping into a pond, the Phantom Sheriff leaped through the fireman's door, hands out-thrust before him.

He landed clear of the uprearing locomotive and skidded thirty feet down a yielding shoulder of sand on the opposite side of the sand dune.

Rolling like a log, Sidlaw brought up short against a bristling thicket of yellow-blossomed prickly pear.

Groaning with shock and the pain of a dozen bruises, Spook Sidlaw kept his eyes open, staring fascinated at the terrible spectacle of the locomotive as it rolled over and over down the slope, flattening dense chaparral as might a steam roller.

The engine tender broke free of its coupling. Coal showered in a black, fan-shaped flood, like dirt from a dynamite blast.

Above the crash of the battered locomotive going over the rimrock into the canyon below, came a thunderous, ear-shattering roar as the boiler burst asunder at every seam, rivets parting as if made of paper.

A final roar, and the smashed locomotive landed in a crushed tangle of iron on the rocks at the pit of the dry gorge.

Steam billowed toward the sky in a vast, blinding white vapor. Scalding clouds blotted out the sun, graying the brassy sky.

For a hundred yards in all direction, stinging

drops of water rained down, peppering Spook Sidlaw's scratched face and raw, bruised hands.

He crawled dazedly out of the cactus, then slumped in exhaustion on the rippled sand dunes.

When his senses cleared, there came to his ears the crackle of burning brush.

Forcing himself to look down the slope toward the brink of the low cliffs where the locomotive had plunged, Sidlaw observed black coils of smoke lifting above the rimrocks, blending with the fuming billows of steam from the smashed boiler.

"Anyway," he panted, "I reckon Jack Shadmer—played out his string—down thar—"

The words sounded ghostly and faraway in Sidlaw's humming ears, as he got shakily to his feet.

Miraculously, he found, he had suffered no broken limbs or ribs. His wild jump for life from the tobogganing locomotive had been successful only because of the sharply reduced speed of the engine and the slanting angle at which he had hit the sand.

Sidlaw peered about him, scenes meeting his eyes in mad, unfocused confusion. A steel rail gleamed in the hillside above him like a twisted piece of rusty wire, torn completely free of the roadbed ties.

The path made by the locomotive in its leap from the tracks had formed an ugly scar down the thick brush that furred the slope of the Dragoon ridge.

A dozen small brush fires smoldered along the mountainside, ignited by live embers thrown from the broken firebox.

Sidlaw took careful stock of his own injuries. His bullhide chaps were torn by sharp rocks and spiny cactus. His Stetson was a battered, shapeless ruin, still clinging to his head because of the frayed chin strap. His boots were ripped at the seams, both spurs had been torn loose when he plowed into the sand.

He crawled into the shade of a silvery-gray smoketree and rested for many minutes, until his laboring heart had settled down to a rhythmic beat and his eyes quit blurring out of focus when he moved them.

The raging brush fire down in the canyon below was burning itself out against the box end of the wash. A desert breeze was thinning the tawny smoke, dissolving the last tatters of steam which still seeped upward out of the canyon.

Sidlaw groped his way down the slope, keeping to the deep furrows plowed out of the hillside by the hurtling locomotive. He clambered over a battered section of the cowcatcher, wedged in an outcrop of quartz. Broken wheels from the ruined coal car lay amid the brush at the chasm's edge.

Making his way to the rimrock, the Phantom

Sheriff stared down into the canyon, shocked at the total destruction he saw there.

The smashed locomotive lay in dense thickets of mesquite and cat's-claw which fire was licking greedily. The boiler was broken and dented like a tin can, flue pipes smoking hotly.

The cab where he and Gila Jack Shadmer had battled was now a splintered, twisted wreck, a full hundred feet from the main part of the locomotive. The engine's wheels, connected by bent drive rods, tilted helplessly toward the skies.

"And somewhar down in that mess, Jack Shadmer's carcass is roastin' to a cinder," muttered Sidlaw, shuddering. "A violent way to cash in—but I cain't rouse much regret about it."

Suddenly nauseated by the horrible sight below, he turned and started toiling back up the slope.

The sound of horses' hoofs drumming the skyline above him made him drop a hand instinctively to the empty holster at his hip.

Then he relaxed. The five horsemen spurring down the hill from the railroad track were friends, members of the Smoketree posse that had been left to make the capture at Gunbore Tunnel.

Sidlaw waved to get their attention, as they dismounted and tied their horses to mesquite clumps farther up the slope.

In the lead came white-headed old Doc Frazer, his horrified gaze reading the grim story of the gouged-out scar down the slope, a gash whose path was scattered with twisted fragments of metal, spilled coal, and other debris from the doomed locomotive.

"As I live an' breathe, if Spook didn't git out o' this alive, gents!" yelled the Malpais County coroner, pointing at the figure of Spook Sidlaw. "No wonder the Mexicans call him the Phantom Sheriff!"

Sammy Duncan, the youthful deputy, was the first to reach Sidlaw. Behind him was Ezra Blaine, boss of the big E Bar B outfit west of Smoketree, and the principal ranch owner in the posse.

"We made a clean sweep, Spook!" cried the deputy sheriff excitedly. "Them Lazy Diamond gunnies surrendered to the last man, back thar in Gunbore Tunnel. Took the fight out o' thar craws when they seen Gila Jack had deserted 'em. We sent Waterbury to release the train crew an' git yore buckskin hoss."

"Yeah," chuckled Doc Frazer, pumping the sheriff's hand. "Congratulations, Spook. Yore scheme worked perfect. Rustlin' is finished in Malpais County now, I reckon—at least so far as Shadmer's operations is concerned."

The coroner looked around questioningly.

"Whar is Shadmer, anyhow?" he demanded.

Sidlaw pointed toward the smoking canyon.

"When the ashes cools down thar, we'll be able

to fish what's left o' Gila Jack Shadmer out o' thar, I reckon," he said. "He was in the engine cab when it shot over the rim an' exploded like a bomb. He didn't have a chance—if he wasn't smashed to a pulp in the crash, he would 'a' scalded to death pronto when that boiler let go."

And then, in taunting contradiction of the evidence, there came to the ears of the men grouped about Sidlaw a high-pitched yell of triumph.

Of one accord, Sidlaw and the Smoketree possemen whirled to stare up the slope.

There, in the act of untying Sammy Duncan's white pony from the group of horses tied to the mesquite bushes, was Gila Jack Shadmer!

Hands flew to holsters. A sharp volley of .45 slugs hammered up at the outlaw, as Shadmer leaped into the saddle and wheeled it about, rearing against the sky.

But the bullets fell short, at that range. Even as the posse members started slogging up the hillside behind the Phantom Sheriff, they saw Gila Jack Shadmer spur over the railroad tracks and vanish from sight on the south side of the ridge.

Sidlaw halted midway up the slope, to point at a series of broken mesquites, bordering the deep gash in the dirt caused by the sledding locomotive.

There were bootprints in the dirt there, and hand tracks where a man had crawled on hands and knees into the thick brush.

"Shadmer jumped out o' that locomotive jest about the time I did, but on the opposite side whar I couldn't see him!" explained the young lawman, pointing to the tracks. "He landed in that brush thar, an' lay doggo all the time I was restin'. An' now he's choused Sammy Duncan's bronc an' vamoosed!"

They climbed wearily to the other horses, thankful that Shadmer, in the haste of his get-away, had not untied and stampeded them.

By the time the men had led their broncs back to the torn-up railroad bed, the escaping outlaw was a dwindling dot on the ridge to the southward. Even while Sidlaw and the dismayed possemen stared, they saw Shadmer dip beyond the horizon.

"Let's go!" bellowed Ezra Blaine. "That's the ringleader o' this rustlin' outfit that's been fleecin' our range fer years. Capturin' him is worth more'n dallyin' our loops on that hull passle o' hired hands down at Gunbore Tunnel!"

But Sidlaw held up a hand, halting their rush for saddles.

"Wait, gents. This ain't no job fer a posse. All we'd do is raise a dust an' give Shadmer plenty o' chances to hide out an' ambush us one by one."

"But," sputtered Doc Frazer impatiently, "he's

kitin' out toward Mexico. Once he crosses the border, he'll be out o' our jurisdiction—"

A strange grin bent Sidlaw's lips as he tapped the gold star he wore—the honorary emblem of a peace officer who was not hampered by man-made boundaries.

"Doc, lend me yore hoglegs. Mr. Blain, kin I borrow yore hoss fer a spell? An' yore saddle rifle?"

The big ranchman handed Sidlaw his reins.

"You aimin' to trail Gila Jack? Why cain't the rest of us j'ine yore party?"

Sidlaw was busy holstering Doc Frazer's twin Colt six-guns.

"Because, as I said, we'd raise too much dust, an' tip off our location to Shadmer. He's desprit. He's headin' fer Mexico, like doc says. But I figger, travelin' alone, I kin overtake Gila Jack. This time I won't figger on bringin' him in alive. We'll shoot it out—finish things in Shadmer's fashion."

Five minutes later, straddling Ezra Blaine's Arabian stock saddle horse, the Phantom Sheriff headed southward along Gila Jack Shadmer's trail, followed by the wistful gazes and hand-waves of farewell of his possemen.

CHAPTER XXII.

Gila Jack Shadmer was still following the rocky ridge of the Dragoon range when sundown overtook him, below the Arizona-Mexico boundary.

Ahead of him, the far-flung expanse of Sonora beckoned, offering danger, yet safety. Those barren, waterless badlands were perilous in themselves, yet they looked like a Garden of Eden to the fugitive killer who for ten years had enjoyed a tyrant's grip on Smoketree and the outlying cattle country.

Somewhere beyond the purple rim of those Mexican highlands, Shadmer would hole up, far out of reach of Arizona law.

Letting his stolen bronc rest, Shadmer twisted in the saddle and peered back over the ground he had traveled. He had put twenty-odd miles of rugged country behind him since his wild flight aboard Sammy Duncan's white pony.

Whispering Desert lay to his left, stretching a hundred miles away from the base of the Dragoons. He could see the spot where Smoketree lay, deep in indigo shadow cast by the mountain.

His face was bitter, but he was taking his loss like the case-hardened gambler he had always been. He had worked hard, risked his hide a thousand times during the years he had struggled to the mastery of his outlaw empire.

He had built the Lucky Dollars Saloon from a filthy shack on Smoketree's main street to the present building, the front of which covered almost a block.

Thousands of dollars, most of them dishonestly won with loaded dice, marked cards, or magnetized roulette wheels, had poured in a never-ending stream into Shadmer's pockets during his years in Smoketree.

He had not hoarded the money, as other cardsharps might have done, for protection against the day when their hands might lose their deftness at cold-decking cards.

Instead, Gila Jack Shadmer had reinvested his cash, pushed the scope of his outlaw interests in ever-widening circles.

The proceeds of one year's cooperation with Francisco Yuma, the Mexican smuggler, had enabled Shadmer to buy up mortgage paper on the Lazy Diamond Ranch, held by the Border State Bank. Shadmer had thus been able to wrest from the rightful owner a ranch which had not been paying well because of drought.

Shadmer had come into possession of a hundred sections of legally-owned cattle range when he had acquired the Lazy Diamond. With the huge spread went the virtual monopoly of Malpais County's teeming cattle business, for Shadmer's ranch flanked the Dragoon range and his control of the Dragoon water rights put other ranchmen at his mercy during dry seasons.

Instead of buying feeder stock from Texas or Montana, Shadmer had hired cowboys who could sling lead as well as twirl a lass' rope. This crew had preyed upon outlying ranches, blotting brands and stealing herds of unbranded cattle outright. South of the border, Shadmer had market connections with unscrupulous Mexicans.

It was a million-dollar empire. Yet Shadmer was fleeing the range where he had been a virtual king, escaping across the border like a cowering saddle tramp.

"An' the skunk who's been responsible fer all this is that Spook Sidlaw hombre," muttered Shadmer bitterly. "Been in town three or four days, an' look at me now—

"It's a cinch I won't ever be able to return to Smoketree, with all they got agin' me," Shadmer went on muttering and groaning. "But some day our trails will cross ag'in, and when they do—"

Shadmer let the threat go unvoiced. Right now, hunger was his main concern. His body was weary from unaccustomed hours in the saddle. His eyes smarted from sun glare, and the coolness of approaching twilight felt good against his sand-blistered face.

He was thankful that Sammy Duncan's horse had proved a good one for rough-country travel.

Not once had the white mustang faltered in the killing pace which Shadmer had set for it. Given hourly rests, the horse still had plenty of stamina left for tomorrow's flight through Mexico.

Shadmer had little fear of pursuit. In the first place, he had a comfortable head start. He had traveled mostly on rocky terrain which would make trailing difficult. But, best of all, he had seen no telltale dust clouds behind him, or other signs of a following posse.

"Reckon I got to go hungry tonight," decided Shadmer, spitting out a dollar cigar because its taste only aggravated his growing appetite. "Reckon by tomorrow noon though, I ought to hit Pozo Verde, whar I kin lay up awhile."

Shadmer had no money worries. In his safe at the Lucky Dollars Saloon in Smoketree, he had upwards of a hundred thousand dollars in *dinero Americano* salted away in gold and greenbacks for just such an emergency as this.

His bartender, Curly Bardoo, would know just where to mail a bundle of currency, whenever Shadmer could get word to him.

Night fell swiftly, once the sunset glow had faded on the cloud banks to westward. In the high altitude of the Dragoons, an icy wind arose which cut through Shadmer's waistcoat and Levi's, making him wish for the warmth of the gambler's blacktailed coat he habitually wore in Smoketree.

He unbuckled one of the saddlebags strapped to Sammy Duncan's kak and extracted therefrom a quart bottle of whiskey. As a rule, Shadmer went light on liquor, knowing that it slowed his trigger finger and dulled his wits when he needed them to be at razor keenness at a big-stake poker game.

Now, gulping down a stiff swig of the whiskey, Shadmer was thankful for the warmth it put in his aching stomach. He dared drink no more, lest the alcohol on his empty stomach make him so giddy-headed he might fall from the saddle and be injured, or left afoot in this barren, uninhabited desert.

His mustang quickened its pace, heading down a long, brushy slope into a cleft between two Dragoons peaks. When the brush thickened, so as to shut off the wind, Shadmer intended to hobble the bronc for the night, wrap himself in the saddle blanket and Sammy Duncan's oilskin slicker, and get some sleep.

"Hoss is hurryin' like mebbe he smelt water," grunted Shadmer, when they were threading through shoulder-high thickets of mesquite and smoketrees. "But thar ain't a spring in this uncurried neck o' the Dragoons that I ever knowed of."

Then Shadmer stiffened in alarm, as his sensitive nostrils brought him the odor of smoke from burning mesquite roots.

"Mexican sheep camp, mebbe," he grunted,

mentally cursing the fact that he had no guns—his own .45s having been hurled from the locomotive by Spook Sidlaw's orders, and Sammy Duncan's saddle being without a booted rifle.

The odor of smoke got stronger. Then, emerging out of the chaparral into a natural clearing, Shadmer reined up sharply as he caught sight of a lonely, flickering campfire.

The gambler slid from the stirrups and put a hand over his stolen mount's nostrils, to prevent the horse from whinnying.

Two men with steeple-peaked sombreros made of pleated palmleaf straw were holding skillets over the little blaze. The tantalizing odor of frying bacon wafted to Shadmer's nostrils.

Behind the campfire was a clump of towering, broken granite, out of which trickled a stream of water to form a pool at the base of the rocks. A pair of burros grazed in the grama grass just outside the ring of firelight.

Were those squatting hombres, with their gun butts projecting from their thighs, men who wore stars? Was this a pair of Arizona Rangers, combing the solitary badlands in search of some owl-hooter such as himself?

Then the crouching outlaw from Smoketree recognized one of the camper's voices raised in raucous song, and he grinned with relief as he placed them.

"Joe an' Jake Kurdle, the desert rat twins!"

186

chuckled the outlaw, striding forward with his horse trailing him. "Many's the time they've likkered up at my bar in Smoketree."

Joe and Jake Kurdle were enigmas around Smoketree. They were seen but once a year, when they drifted out of the Mexican badlands for supplies. Always they paid for their ammunition, foodstuffs and tobacco with gold dust.

Some said the Kurdle twins were loco, driven crazy by their sixty-odd years of prospecting. But mostly they were cagy and eccentric, keeping to themselves, listening much, saying little.

At the sound of Shadmer's approach, Joe and Jake Kurdle laid their frying pans aside and peered about, staring at the tall hombre who walked into range of their firelight.

"*Hola*, Joe an' Jake!" called out the gambler cordially. "Mind if I join yuh? I'm plumb tuckered out. Rid over from Smoketree since three o'clock this afternoon."

The prospectors, both goat-whiskered oldsters in their middle seventies, peered in amazement at their visitor. Usually Gila Jack Shadmer was immaculately dressed, flashy with jewelry.

Now he was ragged and begrimed, the result of his leap for life from the derailed locomotive and his grueling ride through the Dragoons all afternoon.

"Why, shore—hobble yore bronc an' make yoreself to home, Mr. Shadmer," said Jake

Kurdle, hobbling forward to extend a scrawny hand that felt like a bundle of knotty sticks in Shadmer's grasp. "Joe, slice off some more bacon. 'Tain't often we have guests fer supper, Mr. Shadmer."

CHAPTER XXIII.

A good wash at the spring, followed by a meal of sour-dough biscuits, salt beef, bacon, and steaming black coffee, did wonders to Gila Jack Shadmer's appearance and nerves.

His old bearing of arrogance and superiority returned, but he was grateful enough to the pair of desert rats to offer them a pair of crumpled cigars which had been in his vest pocket.

"How come, Mr. Shadmer," queried Joe Kurdle with a toothless grin as he scrubbed a greasy skillet with a tuft of grass roots, "how come yuh're out in this kentry? Yuh look like a hoss throwed yuh an' then a herd o' stampedin' longhorns tromped yuh."

Face wreathed in mellow cigar smoke, Gila Jack decided to invent an explanation for his bruised flesh and torn clothing.

"Yuh're right, Joe. My hoss did throw me, smack into a maguey clump," he grinned ruefully. "Jest as soon lit a nest o' sidewinders. I'm headin' fer Pozo Verde on business."

Joe Kurdle scratched a head as bald as an onion.

"Me an' my brother, Jake, hyar, are makin' our yearly trip to Smoketree an' yore saloon, Mr. Shadmer," the whiskery-faced little prospector explained in his querulous, off-key voice. "Only once a year do we tech whiskey."

Shadmer's beady eyes narrowed thoughtfully. The Kurdle boys had become almost legendary figures in Malpais County history. Upward of forty-five years they had prospected the Dragoons, appearing every twelve months in Smoketree to buy provisions with gold dust, and then get liquored up to the point of total insensibility.

When they sobered, the two gnomelike old brothers would diamond hitch their burros and head off across Whispering Desert for the mountains—to be lost from the eyes of man for another year.

Shadmer's thoughts were racing. If they were on their way to Smoketree now, then they had gold dust with them. And if so, Shadmer intended to possess that gold, before morning.

It was gossiped by talkative barflies and cowboys and Mex peons that the Kurdle twins had located the celebrated Black Padre gold mine—a mine that had been discovered by the ancient Spanish *conquistadores*, a fabulously rich lode supposed to be lost somewhere in the Dragoons.

Shadmer, busy with his gambling, smuggling and cattle rustling enterprises, had never given the Kurdle brothers much thought.

He had refused to give any credence to the

tale about their having rediscovered the Black Padre diggings, known to have been lost for three hundred years. The very existence of the Black Padre mine was, in all probability, merely a wild fable. Yarns about lost mines were rife throughout the West.

"I'll need gold whar I'm goin'," thought Shadmer, eying the six-guns which the Kurdle twins were packing. "May take weeks fer Curly Bardoo to git money to me."

The two prospectors were reputed to be dead shots with the massive, single-action .44s they carried. And Shadmer himself was unarmed.

Then an idea filtered into the gambler's head. He got up, walked over to his saddle, unbuckled one of Sammy Duncan's tooled leather *alforjas*, and drew out the quart whiskey bottle which the deputy sheriff had been carrying.

"In Smoketree they always pass out an' wake up in the jail house after a drinkin' spree," remembered Shadmer, as he walked back to the campfire. "Mebbe I kin git 'em to swig so much o' this rotgut that they'll be easy to handle."

The goat-whiskered prospectors eyed the whiskey bottle with mouths that suddenly drooled. Neither desert rat had tasted a drop in twelve months. The amber bottle in Shadmer's hands would be worth its weight in gold dust to either of the old codgers, and Shadmer knew it.

"I'll give yuh two ounces o' dust fer what's in

that bottle o' snakebite medicine, Mr. Shadmer!" offered Jake Kurdle, pawing in his Levi's and drawing out a buckskin pouch. "With *oro* fetchin' what it is, reckon that's a good price, eh?"

A leering smile twisted Gila Jack Shadmer's lips. He tossed the bottle over to Jake Kurdle and saw him pull out the cork and drink greedily.

"Both of yuh help yoreselves, boys," said the gambler craftily. "I'll be in Pozo Verde tomorrow night, whar I kin git all the redeye I want. Drain 'er to the bottom!"

Joe Kurdle yanked the bottle away from his brother and a moment later his long, scraggly neck was pulsing with each gulp of the fiery bourbon.

"Plumb *bueno*, Mr. Shadmer," cackled Joe Kurdle, passing the bottle back to his brother. "No rotgut in that bottle like yuh peddle acrost the bar at the Lucky Dollars, eh?"

Shadmer puffed his cigar in silence, watching the campfire sparks lift up into the star-dotted sky. He grinned as he saw the two old desert dwellers drain the entire bottle of ninety-proof whiskey, straight.

Once the alcohol got into their bloodstreams, both desert rats would soon pass into a stupor. Then Shadmer knew it would be easy to appropriate their six-guns and take his own time about rifling their packs in search of whatever gold they were carrying.

Jake Kurdle's shirt flared open to expose his

chest as the prospector returned his poke of gold dust to the waistband of his Levi's.

Leaning forward with interest as he watched Kurdle stow the pouch of gold away, Shadmer caught sight of something else which roused his curiosity.

A series of peculiar blue-and-red marks literally covered the prospector's ribs. There were initials and figures tattooed in imperishable ink over his breastbone, reminding Shadmer of a tattooed man he had seen at a road show once.

"What in blazes you got tattooed on yoreself, Jake?" queried the gambler, crossing around to squat beside the tipsy old prospector. "Yuh look like a walkin' map or somethin'."

Jake Kurdle did not realize that Shadmer had used his tattoo markings as an excuse to get closer to him, and snatch the oldster's gun from its holster the moment he saw drunkenness start to overcome the prospector.

" 'Tish a map, Misher Shadmer," was Kurdle's reply, punctuated with loud hiccups. "Map o' how to find a gold mine me an' my twin brother Joe discovered twenty year back."

A gold-mine map! Gila Jack Shadmer's veins raced, as he saw Jake Kurdle open his hickory shirt wider and trace a finger along his tattooed ribs. The firelight showed distinct names tattooed on the amazing map—Dog-ear Butte, Skull Valley, Rio Amargo.

"Thish ish only half the map, though," said Jake Kurdle thickly, his eyes glowing with whiskey-flush. "Joe, over thar, hash a map tattooed on hish brishkit, too. But it'sh a shecret."

Joe Kurdle got up on legs that seemed to be turned to rubber. An angry glare was on his seamed, parchmentlike face as he pawed clumsily at his belt for a six-gun.

"You ain' sh'posed to talk about our mapsh, Jake!" warned Joe Kurdle, his brain addled by whiskey. "Now, we gotta kill thish Misher Shadmer. Nothin'—*hic*—elsh we kin do, now you talked—"

In the nick of time, Gila Jack Shadmer vaulted the campfire and closed a viselike hand on Joe Kurdle's wrist. A short jab to the heart, and the prospector wilted.

Straddling the stunned oldster, Shadmer unbuckled Joe's cartridge belt, whipped it about his own waist, and spun the cylinder of the .44 which Joe had half-removed from his holster.

Jake giggled foolishly at the spectacle, rocking back and forth like an old crone in the glow of the campfire.

"Nobody but the tattoo artist at Nogales knowed about thesh mapsh, Misher Shadmer. An', the artist, he died o' con—*hic!*—consumption. Beshides, we didn't tell him what theshe mapsh wash for anyhow. An' you won't tell our shecret, will yuh, amigo?"

Jack Shadmer composed his face into the expressionless mask he wore at high-stake poker games. Shrewd instinct told him he had stumbled onto something of vital importance. Those tattooed maps might well be worth a million dollars to him.

"Course I won't tell, pardner!" he said, truthfully enough. "That was clever, tattooin' a map thataway. Nobody kin git yore secret as long as it's part o' yore hide, kin they?"

Jake Kurdle laughed uproariously at what he thought humorous.

"That's right. But when yuh find a mine like the Black Padre," he hiccuped, "you *got* to be clever, else every proshpector in Arizona would rush to yore claim. Yeshiree, bob!"

CHAPTER XXIV.

The Black Padre! Gila Jack Shadmer repeated the name softly, wondering whether he could believe his ears. The Kurdle brothers had been rewarded for their patient years of scouring the Dragoons, by finding the long-lost gold diggings of the early Spanish explorers!

Somewhere in these sun-parched Mexican badlands, they had stumbled across the secret diggings of the *conquistadores*. And to guard against the possibility of losing the mine, they had had the brilliant idea of putting a treasure map on their own bodies in the form of indelible tattooing which would go with them to the grave.

Jake Kurdle tried to stand up, but fell heavily across Gila Jack Shadmer. Reaching forward, on the pretenses of supporting the drunken prospector, Shadmer lifted Jake's .44 Colt from its holster.

"Well, I'm goin' to turn in, I reckon," yawned the outlaw. Then, as if by casual afterthought, he asked the bleary-eyed desert rat: "This Black Padre mine of yours—is it far from here?"

Jake Kurdle stiffened warily. His tongue had been loosened by alcohol, but the habit of long years standing now warned him to beware of the leering gambler.

"Thatsh—*hic*—none o' yore bushness, Mish' Shadmer. Me an Joe, we ain' tellin' *nobody*. The Black Padre belongsh to ush, shavvy? We ain' tellin' nothin'."

Jake Kurdle pounded his temples with his palms, as if to shake off the dizziness which had seized him. He was staring with heavy-lidded eyes at his brother, Joe, who, recovering from Shadmer's blow, had gone peacefully to sleep.

"I don't blame yuh fer close-hobblin' yore lip, Jake," agreed Gila Jack Shadmer, standing up and yawning. "Hang on to yore secret as long as yuh kin. Waal, I reckon I'll go out an' see about my bronc's picket pin, an' then turn in. I need some shut-eye bad—because *manana*'s goin' to be a busy day fer me."

The significance of Shadmer's last sentence was lost on Jake Kurdle, as their outlaw guest walked out into the darkness by the spring to where his mount grazed with the prospectors' burros.

Excitement made veins throb in Shadmer's ears. If it were true that Joe and Jake Kurdle had rediscovered the Black Padre mine, Gila Jack Shadmer knew that he had blundered onto a treasure worth far more than the Lazy Diamond Ranch, the Lucky Dollars Saloon, or his other enterprises in Malpais County.

"It'll be a plumb simple matter to salivate them old fogies while they are sleepin' off this drunk, and copy the maps tattooed on their hides," Shadmer told himself. "Once I get that Black Padre mine located, I kin give up the owl-hoot trail, I reck—"

Shadmer broke off, as a nervous whicker from Sammy Duncan's horse warned him that the bronc had spotted something out in the chaparral. A prowling coyote, perhaps, or—

Then, Shadmer's wide-pupiled eyes made out the stalking figure of a sombreroed man, slipping through the buckbrush and mesquites near the granite rise from which the spring water trickled.

The hombre was leading a horse, and kept his hand over the bronc's nostrils to prevent its nickering to the other animals by the waterhole.

Gila Jack drew Jake's .44 Colt and flattened himself against the granite cliff. Who was this stealthy prowler approaching from the north?

Dying firelight twinkled off the brass cartridges which looped the prowler's gun belts, and caught ruby highlights on the horse's bridle trappings.

Whoever it was, the newcomer was making a cautious approach to the desert camp ground.

For several minutes, the visitor crouched with his horse behind a mesquite clump at the edge of the clearing, eyes studying the camp and the two prospectors who lay beside the campfire.

Finally, as if satisfied that no danger awaited him, the horseman stepped out into the open, leading his lather-sided bronc at rein's length.

"*Hola*, the camp!"

Jake Kurdle, who had toppled prone on the ground, propped himself up dizzily, staring about to locate the voice.

Gila Jack Shadmer swore behind clenched teeth, as he recognized that trail-weary voice, recognized the dusty features of the mysterious cowboy who was approaching Kurdle's fire, passing not twenty feet from the spot where Shadmer hid against the dark background of granite.

Slowly, the Smoketree gambler lifted the .44 and lined the sights on the rider's head. For that hombre out of the night who had scouted the camp before declaring himself, was Spook Sidlaw, on whose shirt gleamed the gold badge of the Phantom Sheriff!

CHAPTER XXV.

Pure accident had led Spook Sidlaw to this lonely campfire in the Mexican wilderness.

He had lost the trail of Gila Jack Shadmer an hour before sundown; but reasoning had told him that the escaping outlaw would continue his general southerly flight.

When darkness closed in upon him, Sidlaw was still high on the rocky spine of the Dragoon ridge. From that elevation, he had spotted a tiny pinpoint of light, several miles beyond and below him, in a saddle between sheltering granite peaks.

At last he had worked himself close enough to hear the musical murmur of water trickling out of a pile of granite, and to smell the pungent odor of mesquite roots burning.

"*Hola*, the camp!" the Phantom Sheriff called out, nearing the warmth of the dying campfire.

One goat-whiskered oldster propped himself up on an elbow, and Sidlaw realized from the reek of whiskey that one or both of the prospectors were dead drunk.

"Leavin' ush sho shoon, Mr. Shadmer?" inquired Jake Kurdle, trying to stand up but with dizziness overcoming him. "Thought yuh shaid yuh wash goin' to grab shome shut-eye!"

"Shadmer?"

Cold alarm coursed through Sidlaw as he slapped a hand to his holster, staring wildly about the camp as he did so.

Then, even as he slid a finger into the trigger guard of his Colt, the Phantom Sheriff heard a low, venomous command issue from the neighborhood of the waterhole:

"Paw fer a cloud, Sidlaw! Reckon yuh've stuck yore horns into a trap."

Sidlaw twisted his head. His heart plummeted with despair as he saw the towering form of Gila Jack Shadmer emerge from the shadow-clotted granite wall, and stalk out into the firelight with a Colt .44 jutting from his hip.

Sidlaw dropped his horse's reins and lifted his arms above the battered brim of his Stetson. The horse, free to move away, broke into a trot and headed for the spring, where it drank noisily.

Moving with a gorillalike crouch, Gila Jack Shadmer approached the young lawman, thumb holding the .44 at full cock.

"I'll oblige yuh to unbuckle yore gun harness, Phantom Sheriff!" clipped Shadmer. "And pronto, or I'll gut-shoot yuh."

Moving jerkily, his eyes fixed on the menacing bore of the .44 in Shadmer's hand, Sidlaw fumbled at the buckles of his crisscrossing shell belts, unstrapped them, and dropped them to one side.

Jake Kurdle got to his feet and lurched in a

zigzag away from the campfire. His booze-fuddled brain was puzzled by what was going on.

"Whash matter, Shadmer?" demanded the old desert rat, his shirttails flapping in the night wind. "Whash idea throwin' gun on thish cowhand? He jest wantsh a place to spread hish blanketsh fer the night, like you did—"

Gila Jack Shadmer laughed fiendishly, his eyes never leaving Sidlaw's taut face.

"Me an' this cowpoke got a little grudge to settle, Jake!" Shadmer snarled. "You go over thar by yore blankets an' set quiet. I got a few things to tell this busky afore I put a slug in his belly, an' I don't want no interference from you."

Jake Kurdle tugged at his woolly beard, anger tempering the effects of his whiskey jag.

"Thish ish my camp—an' thash my gun you're usin'!" roared the old desert rat, staggering toward Shadmer. "Give it here, shee? You don't hooraw no cowboy who wantsh to use thish water—"

With cold deliberation, Gila Jack Shadmer swung the .44 toward Jake Kurdle. Sidlaw saw a spurt of orange flame from the muzzle of the Colt, saw the old prospector's lurching approach halted by the jarring impact of a slug on the V of his breastbone.

Crimson appeared on Kurdle's chest. Two threads of blood coursed down his ribs.

Then, with a gagging sound, the oldster pitched flat on his face in the sand at Shadmer's feet.

"Yuh murderin' dog!" said Spook Sidlaw hoarsely, swiveling his gaze over to where Joe Kurdle was sitting up unsteadily. "You didn't have no call to shoot that old-timer down like he was a hydrophoby skunk, Shadmer. Yuh—"

Gila Jack eyed Joe Kurdle warily as the second desert rat weaved his way around the campfire and dropped to his knees beside the motionless corpse of the twin brother who had shared his lonely existence for sixty-odd years.

But Joe Kurdle was too dazed with shock and grief to do anything but stare aghast at his dead brother.

Shadmer turned to the Phantom Sheriff, teeth glittering below a peeled-back upper lip.

"Afore you git yore dose o' lead pizenin', Sidlaw, I got a few things to tell yuh," gritted the outlaw. "Yuh figgered yuh'd roweled me out o' Malpais County, didn't yuh? Yuh kilt Francisco Yuma an' busted our smugglin' ring. Yuh took my Lazy Diamond spread away from me yesterday. Yuh figgered yuh had me licked, didn't yuh?"

Sidlaw shrugged.

"Yuh're top dog tonight, Shadmer. Yuh talk big when yuh hold the drop. But yuh'll never be able to show yore mangy hide around Smoketree ag'in, Gila Jack. Knowin' that won't make dyin' so hard for me to face."

Shadmer's eye dropped to a pair of nickel-plated handcuffs which were looped over the cowboy lawman's belt. Those fetters had once been the property of Sheriff Buck Clawson, and Shadmer knew that the Phantom Sheriff had carried them out to the railroad on Whispering Desert the day before with the intention of locking them about Shadmer's wrists.

Now the tables were reversed, and an evil plan was born in Shadmer's hate-filled brain.

"Keep yore hands stretchin' high, Phantom Sheriff," warned the outlaw, approaching him warily. "I'm honin' to git at them bracelets o' Buck Clawson's."

Sidlaw felt the hard pressure of Shadmer's gun in the pit of his stomach as the gambler lifted the handcuffs from his belt.

"Now, lower yore arms an' put yore wrists together."

Shadmer clicked one cuff about Sidlaw's right wrist, then snapped the other about his left wrist.

"You ever heard o' the Black Padre gold mine, busky?" asked Shadmer, eying his handcuffed prisoner sharply.

Sidlaw nodded, puzzled by his captor's abrupt change of subject.

Although born and bred in the Thundergust Valley country up in Wyoming, Sidlaw had often heard of the legendary Black Padre diggings. It was one of the more famous of the lost mine fables which had circulated the length and breadth of the Western frontier.

"Reckon I have, Shadmer. What's the Black Padre mine got to do with you hogtyin' me?"

Shadmer jerked his head over to where Joe Kurdle was still staring in frozen horror at the corpse of his murdered brother.

"Waal, these two jaspers discovered the Black Padre, Sidlaw. Names are Joe an' Jake Kurdle, an' they been prospectin' the Dragoons fer fifty years or more."

The Phantom Sheriff listened in rapt attention.

"I got 'em drunk tonight, intendin' to git their guns away from 'em, an' their pokes o' gold dust. Instead, they loosened their tongues an' told me about a map tattooed on their chests—one half of it on Jake's body, the other half on Joe's. All I got to do is foller that map, an' the Black Padre gold will be mine!"

Cold dismay replaced the sullen anger in the Phantom Sheriff's heart, as he realized why Shadmer was taking his banishment from Smoketree so casually.

"Come daylight, I'm goin' to locate that Black Padre mine—it must be somewhar's close about. An' I'll live in comfort the rest o' my life, Sidlaw—thanks to you chasin' me out o' Malpais County. You brung me good luck, Phantom Sheriff—*muchas gracias*!"

A snarl of anger from Joe Kurdle interrupted

Shadmer. He spun around, to see Joe Kurdle approaching him with a hand ax clutched in bony fists.

Joe was cold sober now. A murderous light glowed in his narrowset eyes as he approached Shadmer, swinging the ax in glittering arcs.

"What's eatin' yuh, yuh old goat?" growled Shadmer, hefting the .44 in his hand.

"You kilt my brother!" snarled the whiskery-faced old codger in a voice which showed no trace of drunkenness. "Yuh got our secret from him. But yuh ain't goin' to live to locate our Black Padre—"

Joe Kurdle swung back the hand ax, intending to hurl it tomahawk-fashion at the leering gambler.

But with a harsh laugh of scorn, Gila Jack pounced upon the scrawny old desert rat even as Kurdle hauled back the ax. Firelight glinted on the blue barrel of the Colt .44, and the steel thudded soddenly across Joe's egg-bald skull.

Knocked cold, the second Kurdle twin flopped in his tracks, dropping the ax on the legs of his murdered brother.

CHAPTER XXVI.

Shadmer wiped a crimson smear from the barrel of the Colt and glanced over at the Phantom Sheriff.

"I dassn't kill this old goat until I've located the mine fer shore," he explained. "An' I've figgered out how I'm goin' to kill you, Sidlaw. In fact, I ain't goin' to kill yuh at all. I'm goin' to let Jake Kurdle's burro kill yuh, come mornin'!"

Sidlaw frowned with puzzlement at the killer's strange words, as Shadmer crossed over to where his own saddle lay and returned with a Manilla lariat.

"I need some shut-eye, so I'm tyin' you to that manzanita tree until daylight," Shadmer explained, dropping the noose over Spook's body and trussing his arms tight to his sides. "I got to make shore that burro is plenty thirsty, afore he kills yuh."

Sidlaw stooped to tie the Phantom Sheriff's legs together at the knees. Then he hauled the rope sharply and pulled his victim off his feet.

Dragging Sidlaw like a hogtied calf, the gambler crossed the camp ground to where a red-barked manzanita stood. Then he lifted his prisoner so that his back stood to the bole of the desert tree and lashed the remaining length of the riata in such fashion that Sidlaw was tied in a standing position facing the campfire, his back to the tree trunk, so tightly bound that he could scarcely move.

"After Jake's burro has killed yuh, Sidlaw, the coyotes an' *zopilotes* will find yuh pronto," chuckled Shadmer. "It's a cinch no human bein' will pass by. The Kurdle boys told me at supper tonight that nobody ever travels this way. The existence o' this waterhole ain't even known to anybody but the Kurdle twins."

Shadmer went over to Joe Kurdle's insensible form and tied him up with a rawhide rope taken from one of the diamond-hitched packs.

That done, Shadmer hauled off his boots and chaps and crawled between the blankets which Jake Kurdle had spread for his own bed. But now Kurdle was stiffening in death, a few feet away.

"*Buenos noches*, Sidlaw!" yawned the Smoke-tree killer, rolling over in the soogans. "See yuh in the mornin'. Don't go 'way!"

Whereupon Shadmer dropped off to sleep, his snores coming with monotonous regularity.

The Phantom Sheriff groaned as he tried to move an arm or leg. But it was useless. To move only added to the discomfort of the tight bonds which held him to the manzanita. He realized, with a pang of despair, that escape would be impossible during the hours that Shadmer would be sleeping.

"What in blazes has Shadmer got in mind fer me, anyhow?" Sidlow asked himself. "Talks about Jake Kurdle's burro goin' to kill me, an' all that! What kind o' play is Shadmer ribbin' up, anyhow?"

Finally sleep came to Spook Sidlaw. Tortured sleep, in which he dreamed repeatedly that Marie Clawson and old Doc Frazer passed by the camp, but his throat was paralyzed so that he could not scream out for help.

Each time he would rouse himself from the nightmare, to find himself bathed with damp sweat. Each time he would see Gila Jack Shadmer snoring in his blankets, and the ashes of the dead campfire, and the stiffening corpse of Jack Kurdle.

The cold icy wind was stiffening Sidlaw's muscles, adding to his intense discomfort. The night breeze was moaning a death knell through the rustling foliage of the manzanita behind him.

But the doomed cowboy was exhausted by his hard trek across the Dragoons, and sleep came at last, sleep untormented by dreams.

The noise of Gila Jack Shadmer chopping wood for a breakfast fire roused Spook Sidlaw, just as the eastern horizon was turning pink to promise an early sunrise.

In spite of the numbness of his body, sleep had refreshed the Phantom Sheriff.

Joe Kurdle was conscious once more, his eyes

alternating between his brother's corpse and Gila Jack Shadmer, who was frying bacon and boiling coffee before a rousing campfire.

Occasionally the prospector's gaze would drift over to the prisoner tied to the manzanita, and his eyes would flash a mute message of sympathy to his companion in despair.

Gila Jack Shadmer wolfed a hearty breakfast. Then he propped Joe Kurdle to a sitting position on the ground and fed him bacon and a cup of coffee.

"We start huntin' fer the Black Padre today," said the outlaw. "Jake's got the first half o' that treasure map on him, so I'll copy that. But if I have trouble decipherin' the map on yore chest, yuh kin help me."

Joe Kurdle mumbled an oath under his beard.

"I'll die afore I show yuh whar the Black Padre is!" he spat defiantly. "I'm keepin' my trap close-hobbled."

Shadmer grinned.

"Thar's ways o' makin' yuh talk," he said, leering.

So far, Gila Jack had ignored the Phantom Sheriff. He rummaged through the Kurdle brother's packs, loading food supplies on Joe's burro and paying no attention to their mining tools.

Jake Kurdle's burro was picketed some distance from the waterhole, and the little animal brayed raucously as it saw Shadmer allow its mate to drink.

Spook Sidlaw watched curiously as Shadmer saddled up Sammy Duncan's white pony and lifted Joe Kurdle astride behind the cantle. Then he tied the miner's ankles together under the pony's belly.

The Phantom Sheriff noticed that the horse he had borrowed from Ezra Blaine was nowhere in sight. He had not seen the bronc since the night before. Probably it was out grazing in the chaparral somewhere around the camp.

"Now to copy Jake's map—"

Gila Jack Shadmer took an envelope from his pocket, squatted beside Jake Kurdle's gruesome form, shooed flies from the bullet wound and puffed callously on a cheroot as he copied the tattooed treasure map on the corpse's chest.

"Judgin' from this map, the trail leads south along this ridge, which same means that the Black Padre mine is deeper in Mexico than I figgered," Shadmer observed, as he pocketed his copy of the map. "That makes it all the better. I kin do my gold grubbin' without havin' to worry about gringo sheriffs findin' me."

Shadmer stood up, glancing over at the Phantom Sheriff for the first time. Sidlaw recoiled under Shadmer's murderous stare.

"I reckon Jake's burro is perty thirsty by now, Sidlaw," announced the Smoketree gambler. "His bein' thirsty is what's goin' to croak you, amigo. But afore he does, yuh'll have plenty o' time to regret havin' come to Smoketree to help Buck Clawson tie a knot in my tail."

Sidlaw felt a chill ripple down his back. What was Shadmer driving at? What connection would a thirsty burro have with the murder scheme that Shadmer had plotted?

He was not long in finding out.

The sun was just lifting above the horizon when Gila Jack Shadmer walked over to Jake Kurdle's burro and pulled the picket pin. Then, instead of allowing the burro to rush over to the spring to slack its thirst, Shadmer pulled the protesting little animal over to the manzanita where Sidlaw was tied.

Releasing the Phantom Sheriff from the tree, Shadmer lifted the burro, his booted legs almost touching the ground.

So sore and weak was Sidlaw from his night's ordeal that he could not summon the strength to resist as Gila Jack Shadmer cut a small piece of rope and tied his ankles together under the burro.

That done, Shadmer took the hand ax with which he had chopped fuel for the breakfast fire, and drove the picket pin in the hard soil some forty feet distant from the waterhole.

Immediately the burro headed for the spring to drink, thinking he was loose. But the picket rope brought him up short.

"I don't savvy," growled Joe Kurdle huskily. "Yuh aimin' on starvin' this pore rannihan to death, along with the burro?"

Shadmer laughed harshly.

"Not exactly," he said. "Watch an' see."

Shadmer obtained another lariat from Jake Kurdle's diamond-hitched pack. He pulled a noose through the brass hondo and passed the slipknot over Sidlaw's head, adjusting it on the cowboy's neck.

The other end of the rope he tied securely to the manzanita, in such a way as to leave considerable slack on the ground. Lastly, he reset the picket pin to give more slack.

"Now yuh git the idea, amigos?" taunted Shadmer, stepping back to survey his handiwork. "The burro will git to wantin' water powerful bad, once the sun gits to beatin' down on him. But when he walks toward the waterhole, the rope dallied around the Phantom Sheriff's neck will reach the end of its slack an' choke him, squeezin' tighter the more the burro tries to git to that water. Eventually it'll break Sidlaw's mangy neck fer him."

Panic sent a shudder through the Phantom Sheriff as he realized at last the meaning behind Shadmer's mysterious activities.

The burro was standing docile now, flap ears dejected, head bogged down until its muzzle touched the ground. But when blazing sunlight intensified its thirst, the burro would move toward the spring. And before he came to the end of his picket rope, the slipknot about Sidlaw's neck would come taut and strangle him.

"No use wastin' any more time, I reckon," guffawed Shadmer, mounting Sammy Duncan's pony and gathering up the reins. "I got that Black Padre mine to locate today. Adios—see yuh in hell, Sidlaw!"

CHAPTER XXVII.

Horror froze Sidlaw's veins as he watched Gila Jack Shadmer canter off into the chaparral, consulting his scribbled treasure map as he roweled the white pony out of a trot.

Joe Kurdle, seated behind the outlaw, twisted about to call a hoarse farewell to his partner in torture.

Then they were gone.

"Shadmer," moaned the Phantom Sheriff, "dealt from the bottom o' the deck, as usual. Even if a man held a royal flush, Shadmer would bob up with five aces an' win the pot!"

The ruddy globe of the lifting sun threw long shadows over the camp ground where death had visited the night before. Bluebottle flies buzzed noisily as they crawled over Jake Kurdle's stark corpse.

The campfire crackled, but Sidlaw noticed that its smoke was thin and colorless, fading before it had lifted above the chaparral. No hope that the rising column of smoke would attract any desert traveler, even if such existed in this arid, trackless region.

A rattlesnake slithered into a crack in the granite cliffs. A road runner, made bold by the departure of the two campers and seeing no visible sign of life about, drank briefly at the spring and then flew away to its nest in some cactus plant.

A deathly silence descended over the camp, broken only by the babble of water sluicing down the rocks and the breathing of the burro.

"When this critter starts movin' ag'in," moaned the Phantom Sheriff, "it'll be taps fer me. Handcuffed, an' tied, an' no chance o' anybody passin' by—"

Even as he spoke, the burro lifted its head, peered lazily about. Shifting wind brought the smell of cool, fresh water to the beast once more.

The same breeze wafted smoke from the campfire into the burro's nostrils, lifting upward to make Spook Sidlaw blink his eyes.

"By gosh—that smoke gives me an idea!" Sidlaw cried, straightening up. "I jest wonder—"

He twisted to scan the rope which led from the burro's halter to the deep-driven picket pin. It had plenty of slack, but the rope would be a full ten feet short of allowing the burro to reach the nearest edge of the pool. Shadmer had made certain of that, for it was the key to his whole murderous scheme.

Then Sidlaw scanned the lariat which led from the manzanita to his own throat, mentally figuring it slack.

"By gosh—there's a chance my scheme'll work—providin' I kin persuade this fool burro to stop when I want him to!"

The burro, as if taking its rider's speech for a go-ahead signal, lifted its flap ears and started at an ambling walk toward the nearby spring. He detoured instinctively from the campfire which lay in his path.

Peering behind him at the two ropes which the burro was trailing, Spook Sidlaw watched until the picket rope and his own neck rope were poised above the campfire.

The time had come for his own faint chance at escape.

"Whoa! Whoa up, burro!" he shouted.

But the burro, believing it was free to head for the water to quench its night's thirst, was not to be halted by a vocal order. And, without a bridle or any other way of controlling the burro's halter, Sidlaw knew he had to think fast. Another couple of yards and the burro would have taken up the slack of the rope.

The dumb brute would not stop until it reached the end of its own picket rope. And by that time, Shadmer's diabolical trap would have claimed its victim—the shorter hangrope would have tightened to choke the life from his body.

Then, in a wild flood of inspiration, when mere seconds of time remained before the choke rope tightened, Spook Sidlaw toppled himself sideways off the burro's back.

His legs, tied together at the ankles, held him

with knee clamping the burro's ribs, even as his head and shoulders struck the sandy soil.

Sidlaw wedged one shoulder into the dirt as the burro dragged him forward. He felt a sharp jerk at the hondo around his neck, knew he was fighting against time as well as inches of slack rope.

Frantically he jerked his legs down so that they impeded the movement of the burro's hips. The little pack animal halted, peering back at the unaccustomed obstacle which was entangling its hind hoofs.

For a dozen seconds, the Phantom Sheriff waited for the burro to either start trying to buck off his burden, or start kicking at him with sharpedged hoofs.

Instead, the lazy-tempered beast halted and slumped over on one hip, once more bogging its head downward.

Hope warmed the Phantom Sheriff's heart as he lay with one shoulder gouged into the dirt, his trussed ankles over the burro's hip bones and rump, his head in the shadow of the animal's belly.

His eye traveled along the line of the burro's slack picket rope, and his own neck rope.

Both ropes had sagged into the middle of the burning fire!

"If this jack will only stand still another minute—"

Sidlaw's words were a fervent prayer as he stared at the ropes hanging in the campfire. The odor of burning horsehair came from the picket rope. Blending with it was the smell of burning Manilla hemp, as the flames bit into the strands of the lariat about Sidlaw's neck.

Suspense made Sidlaw's heart pound. Blood rushed to his head, tom-tommed in his ears. How long he could depend on the sluggish burro standing still, he did not know.

But years of work with the Kurdle Brothers had taught the sleepy-tempered burro plenty of patience. What manner of strange obstacle was harnessed to his back and impeding his hind legs, the burro did not know.

It chose to wait, in the manner of its breed, eyes half closed, ears flopped in mulish relaxation.

Minutes passed, as flames steadily devoured the two ropes lying in the campfire. Finally, after an eternity of suspense, Sidlaw saw the Manilla lass' rope sag, felt the pressure of the loop about his neck lessen as the rope broke in two.

" 'Sta bueno—move along, burro!" cried the waddy, knocking his knees against the burro's flanks and struggling to shove his shoulders away from the burro's legs. "Reckon you can snap that picket rope now!"

It was true. The burro, bucking forward, brought the charred horsehair rope taut.

There was a snapping sound as fire-eaten

horsehair braids parted under the pull of the burro.

A moment later the little beast of burden was shuffling toward the spring unhindered by binding ropes, while Spook Sidlaw struggled along in a series of jouncing movements, fighting to keep his face from dragging on the ground and his body getting in the way of the burro's hoofs.

The burro halted at the edge of the spring and plunged its muzzle into the cool, sparkling water.

Desperately, Spook Sidlaw started pulling hard against his right boot, as the germ of another plan came into his mind.

Bit by bit, he felt his socked foot slipping out of the boot, which was tied to his other ankle across the top of the burro's rump.

With a final jerk, Sidlaw's leg came free of the boot, and his other foot dropped free. He was safe!

"Whew—reckon this is my lucky day!"

The Phantom Sheriff rolled away from the burro and stood up. His left leg was still incased in a cow boot, the other boot dragging by a section of rope.

But the hardest part was over, now.

Kneeling alongside the burro, the Phantom Sheriff sucked in several mouthfuls of reviving water.

Refreshed by the cool liquid, the cowboy walked over to the spot where Gila Jack Shadmer had tossed aside the ax with which he had driven the burro's picket pin.

Kneeling, he managed to get his fingers about the handle of the ax. By twisting the blade upward, he was able to rub its keen edge against the ropes which held his arms to his sides.

The work was tedious and agonizingly slow. His body ached from the cramped effort. But time meant nothing to a man who had tottered on the brink of eternity as he had done.

How long it took for the blade to sever the rope, Sidlaw never knew. But when his arms came loose and the bonds unwound, he stood up and breathed with relief.

His handcuffs presented no problem; Shadmer had not taken his keys. It was clumsy work ferreting the key out of his chaps pocket, but once he had done so he placed the key in his teeth and made short work of unlocking first one manacle, then the other.

"By golly, Freddie Clawson's gold badge must have good luck connected with it," Sidlaw muttered, grinning, as he belted the handcuffs and began massaging his puffed and bleeding wrists. "A real phantom couldn't 'a' managed much better."

The sleepy-mannered burro had finished drinking, and now, finding himself untethered, kicked up defiant heels and galloped out of sight in the chaparral.

Sidlaw watched the burro's departure with intense regret, for it meant he was stranded in the middle of parched desert, a good fifty miles by crow's flight from Smoketree. He knew it would be impossible to catch the burro now; it would become a wild thing of the desert.

His aching stomach reminded him of the necessity of getting food into his body. He rummaged through the scattered packs of the Kurdle twins, trying to keep his gaze away from Jake's corpse.

He came across some moldy sour-dough biscuits which Gila Jack Shadmer had disdained to take along. The food, poor as it was, put new life in the waddy's jaded frame as he washed the hard biscuits down with spring water.

"I'll have to hoof it back to Smoketree an' report failure to Marie Clawson, I reckon," he muttered. "But with the town behind me like it is, I reckon I kin call my job finished an' kin return this gold star to Marie. She—"

Sidlaw broke off with a start of horror as he heard the clatter of a horse approaching. Before he could move to hide, the horse emerged from the chaparral.

But it was not Gila Jack Shadmer returning to investigate his murder trap. It was Ezra Blaine's mustang, which the Phantom Sheriff had turned loose the night before at the time of his capture.

The horse, coming back to the waterhole after a night of foraging, was a welcome sight to a waddy who had contemplated the grueling trek back to Smoketree afoot.

Almost as welcome a sight was that of the Winchester .30-30 which still reposed in Blaine's saddle boot.

Sight of that carbine put a new idea into the Phantom Sheriff's head.

"If I kin find food, I'll be able to track Gila Jack afore his trail gits too cold!" cried Sidlaw excitedly. "I kin copy the first half o' that treasure map offn Jake's corpse, as well as Gila Jack did—"

He caught the horse while it was drinking and tied it to the manzanita, stripping off the saddle for the horse's comfort.

Then he returned to finish inspecting the packs which Gila Jack Shadmer had torn to pieces in his search for whatever gold dust the Kurdle twins might have been carrying.

The hunt disclosed a sack of parched corn and a tin of chipped beef—rations for a day or so of travel, when augmented by filled canteens from the nearby spring.

"With luck, I could overtake Gila Jack an' Joe Kurdle afore sundown," muttered the Phantom Sheriff. "But first, I guess I owe a duty to Jake Kurdle, here."

Sidlaw picked up a prospector's shovel and dug a shallow grave.

Then he copied the tattooed map on Jake

Kurdle's chest, to assist him in trailing Jack Shadmer on the latter's quest of the Black Padre diggings.

"Adios, old-timer," whispered Sidlaw, as he rolled Jake's body in a tarp and laid it in the grave. "Here's hopin' I kin reach yore brother afore Shadmer croaks him, too."

Sidlaw covered the grave with a cairn of rock to keep away marauding timber wolves.

Then he resaddled his mustang, inspected the ammunition in the .30-30's magazine, and headed southward, following the tracks of Gila Jack Shadmer's stolen horse.

CHAPTER XXVIII.

Nightfall overtook Gila Jack Shadmer and his prisoner, Joe Kurdle, making camp in a sandy basin surrounded by treeless ridges.

All through the day Shadmer had zigzagged from landmark to landmark, following the direction of the tattoo map he had copied from Jake Kurdle's chest.

The final landmark on this map was called "Skull Valley" on the tattoo, and Shadmer was positive this sandy basin was that goal. In general shape the basin resembled a human skull, and to heighten the illusion there were a pair of volcanic cinder cones, common to that section of Sonora, spaced near the top half of the pear-shaped valley and resembling eye sockets in a skull.

Using provisions stolen from the prospectors, Shadmer cooked a meal, sharing part of it with Joe Kurdle. The trussed prisoner ate in moody silence. Throughout the day, the bald-headed little prospector had kept his lips clamped tight, refusing to talk.

The meal completed, Shadmer spread a bedroll, dividing the blankets with Joe Kurdle. The desert man snarled in baffled fury as Shadmer ripped off his blue jean shirt to study the tattoos on his chest.

"From now on we travel on this map o' yourn," said Shadmer, scanning the tattooing by the firelight. "Seems like Dog-ear Butte is the next landmark we want."

Shadmer's eyes ranged over the horizon, spotting almost instantly a prominent peak with two small crags at its crest.

"That butte looks like a dog's head with ear stickin' up. You boys shore named landmarks plumb *bueno*, didn't yuh? If I knowed fer shore I could foller yore map this easy, I'd leave yuh fer buzzard bait to keep from ridin' double."

That night the outlaw's dreams were filled with visions of long-lost Spanish gold—gold that would be his, probably on the morrow.

They were on the trail to Dog-ear Butte before the sun rose next day. A two-hour ride brought them to the butte, and the next landmark, according to the treasure map tattooed on Joe Kurdle's scrawny ribs, would be a river which snaked its way southwesterly into the Sonora wastelands.

"*Rio Amargo*—Bitter River," translated the gambler, spurring his hoof-weary bronc across the shoulder of Dog-ear Butte. "An' accordin' to yore map, Joe, we'll be findin' the Black Padre mine somewhar near the forks o' that river. That ought to be easy—but I ain't killin' yuh till we actually gits thar."

From the high elevation accorded by the butte,

the canyon of the Rio Amargo was clearly visible until it petered out on a range of broken hills which the Kurdle brothers had named *Sierra Fornallo*—Furnace Mountain.

A greedy light kindled in Gila Jack Shadmer's red-shot eyes as they pushed on across the barren desert country. Somewhere on the gashed, rocky slopes of Furnace Mountain he would find the long-lost Spanish gold of ancient times, he felt positive.

They reached the entrance of Bitter River's gorge at noon. Heat reflected from the red volcanic cliffs, as if they were the sides of a bake oven.

But the glittering water which swashed over the rapids below sounded like music to the ears of the tired horse.

Shadmer flung himself from the saddle as they reached the water's edge. Scooping the cold liquid into his palms, Gila Jack drank greedily.

Tied aboard the white pony, Joe Kurdle threw back his head and laughed triumphantly as he saw the Smoketree killer spit the water out, grimacing from the salty chemicals which rendered the water unfit to drink.

"Bitter River, eh?" cursed Shadmer, rinsing out his mouth with the last of the canteen water they carried. "I'd jest as soon try to swig down a bottle o' ink."

The water was useful for bathing his face and

cooling the mount's saddle sores, however.

That done, they moved on down the canyon, following a barren ledge which bore no marks of previous travel.

More and more, as Shadmer penetrated deeper into the Black Padre's vicinity, he realized the necessity of using a map to find the lost gold mine.

The rocky soil left no tracks to follow. And, owing to the broken contour of the wilderness, some sort of chart was absolutely essential to keep from becoming hopelessly lost.

Spurring the double-laden bronc relentlessly, Shadmer pushed on and on through the searing heat of Bitter River's twisting canyon, which lifted gradually as it shortened the height of its granite walls.

Mid-afternoon brought them to the forks of Bitter River, where Joe Kurdle's map ended. A ledge led to the rimrock, and Shadmer spurred up to find himself on the bleak side of Furnace Mountain, faced by an endless expanse of country as dead as if it were on the moon.

A thousand barrancas had eroded into the face of the mountain. There was no prominent landmark to be seen in the heat-dancing atmosphere.

They had reached dead end. That meant that the Black Padre mine was somewhere close by. But where? It might be inside one of the nearby gulches which furrowed the slope. But perhaps it was fifty miles away, in any direction of the compass. Perhaps the Kurdle twins employed their tattooed maps to get this close, and depended on memory to get the rest of the way to the gold mine.

Gila Jack Shadmer dismounted and peered up at Joe Kurdle, sitting slumped over behind the cantle.

"Now's the time, Joe," rasped the outlaw, "to make *hable*. Unless you talk, I won't be able to find the Black Padre, an' you know it. So I intend to make you talk."

The old prospector returned Shadmer's snakelike gaze without flinching.

"Speak up!" raged Shadmer, drawing a six-gun. "Whar do we go next?"

Kurdle licked his black, swollen lips, seamed with fiery red cracks where the penetrating sunshine had split the tissues. There was a triumphant gleam in the old prospector's faded eyes which Gila Jack Shadmer did not like.

"Shore I'll talk, Shadmer. Shore I'll tell yuh whar the Black Padre is. But yuh're in fer a dose o' bitter medicine, yuh snake-hearted polecat."

Surging dismay throbbed up in Shadmer's throat. Kurdle's voice carried the ring of sincerity, of triumph.

"What you drivin' at, Joe? You trick me, an' I'll

229

burn yuh at a stake like an Apache would, blast yore shriveled hide!"

Joe Kurdle pointed his head toward a nearby canyon mouth.

"The Black Padre mine is inside o' that gulch whar all the ocotillo cactus is growin', Shadmer. But yuh won't find any gold in it. Durin' all the years Jake an' me worked that mine, we didn't find any gold in the mine itself."

"Meanin' what?"

"Meanin' that them Spanish padres worked the vein till it petered out—else why did they leave it? The gold me an' Jake got we picked out o' the mine tailin's—particles too tiny fer the ol' padres to worry about."

Shadmer's face mottled with rage.

"You're lyin', Joe. That mine was the richest one the Spanish explorers ever found. Some earthquake or somethin' caused it to be lost—"

Joe Kurdle shook his bald head. His eyes twinkled in obvious enjoyment of Shadmer's discomfiture.

"Shore—it *was* a rich mine. But the Spaniards cleaned it slicker'n a hound's tooth. Me an' Jake finished up the tailin's last spring. Did yuh stop to ask yoreself why we was carryin' picks an' shovels when you found us? If we had a gold mine to work, we'd have left our tools at the Black Padre, wouldn't we?"

Horror—black, corroding horror—was eating

Gila Jack Shadmer as he admitted to himself that Kurdle's words were convincing.

"We left the Black Padre months ago. It's jest a dead bunch o' tunnels, Shadmer. Take it—an' welcome to it. Jest remember, afore yuh shoot me, that he who laughs last—"

Gila Jack's curse cut off Joe Kurdle's taunting words. The outlaw jabbed his gun into holster, reached for the bridle reins and tied them to a dead pinon nearby.

"I aim to find out if you tricked me into this country on a wild-goose chase, Joe!" screamed Shadmer in a voice like a maniac's. "I'm goin' up to that gulch, an' see if that mine's there. If it is—an' if I don't see any gold—I'm comin' back an' beat you to death with my gun butts!"

Disregarding the blistering heat, which made his heart pound overfast, Gila Jack Shadmer sprinted up the flinty slope, his keen eyes observing the rock chips which had obviously been dumped here by a wheelbarrow.

He struggled through dense thickets of ocotillo and ignota brush, scaring a red-necked buzzard who had been feasting on a dead coyote.

Breaking through the brush, Shadmer halted, eyes bulging from their sockets as he spied a low, cavelike opening at the base of the cliff. It was a tunnel braced with ancient timbers, barely as high as a man's head.

Carved in the rock above the tunnel mouth

was a date more than three hundred years old—the work of some Spaniard's chisel in ancient times.

But weeds now masked the rock chips underfoot. There was no evidence that the Kurdle boys had worked here in recent months.

Babbling an inarticulate cry, Gila Jack Shadmer slogged forward, peering into the black maw of the long-lost cavern, he saw a rusty old wheelbarrow, a lantern hanging from a nail driven into a ceiling timber, and some cast-off clothing.

"Then—it's true! It's true! This mine ain't nothin' now but a hole in the ground. It ain't got any more value than a skunk's den!"

Cold fury flooded Gila Jack Shadmer. Whatever he did in the way of revenge against Joe Kurdle, he knew that Joe Kurdle was the real victor. For Gila Jack Shadmer knew he could never get out of these grim badlands alive. Lack of food and water would turn him into a raving madman.

Turning away from the Black Padre tunnel, Gila Jack Shadmer lowered his black Stetson brim and pushed back through the cactus until he came to the open.

Suddenly berserk, he ran down the rubble-carpeted hillside to where Joe Kurdle sat slumped like a straw-stuffed dummy on the white horse.

"Joe—I'll torture you fer this!"

Kurdle did not answer. There was something

strangely awful about the way his bald head had toppled forward over a warped chest. Something spectral in the relaxed old hands.

"Joe—"

But Gila Jack Shadmer knew instinctively that he was speaking to a dead man. Joe Kurdle's stout old heart had given out, his frail body unable to endure the grueling punishment which Shadmer's capture had meted out.

And in death, Joe Kurdle had cheated Shadmer out of the only satisfaction that remained—the satisfaction of seeing the wrinkled old body writhe in torture.

Overcome with savage, insane fury, Gila Jack Shadmer whipped out his twin .45s and started riddling the old man's corpse with slugs.

Echoes fled out over the sweltering air, as Shadmer jerked triggers in fiendish abandon until the firing pins snapped on empty cartridges.

CHAPTER XXIX.

Spook Sidlaw halted his jaded horse in Bitter River Canyon at the point where the stream divided into two forks.

He shoved back his Stetson and cuffed sweat from a hot brow.

"We're perty shore Shadmer come down this canyon, hoss," Sidlaw grunted huskily to his dejected mount, "but whether he went out any o' the side ravines is another thing ag'in. An' here the canyon forks. Which way should we take?"

He had, more or less, been following a blind hunch ever since he had left Skull Valley early that morning.

The copy of the map he had copied from Jake Kurdle's corpse the day before, had taken him almost to Skull Valley before night had overtaken him and forced him to camp.

As he was crossing Skull Valley shortly after daylight that morning, he came across a still-smoking campfire, and plenty of tracks. This was heartening to the trail-weary waddy; it meant he was gaining on Shadmer and Joe Kurdle.

There had been a visible trail to follow to the edge of Skull Valley. That trail had led in the general direction of a twin-peaked butte on the southwestern horizon.

Since his map ended at Skull Valley, Sidlaw knew he would have to rely on his tracking ability from now on. But the tracks petered out on the rocky soil before he had reached the butte.

From the butte he had spotted the winding canyon of Bitter River, though he had no way of knowing it by name. There was a distinct probability that the trail to the Black Padre mine went through that canyon, it being by far the most prominent feature of the Mexican landscape.

Accordingly, he had followed the alkaline river for hours. He was reassured that he was on the right track from time to time by finding fresh hoofprints on mud bars, or the scratches of steel horseshoe calks on granite.

Now he had reached the fork in the river, and for the past five miles he had cut no sign to indicate that Shadmer and Kurdle had not left the canyon at some point behind him.

Then, even as he held the reins in confusion as to which fork to take, the stillness was shattered into a thousand bits by a clatter of gunfire.

Fast-triggered shots, as evenly spaced as the blows of a hammer, crashed in flat, ear-jarring echoes against the cliffs above him. They seemed to come from the north rimrock.

Sidlaw dismounted, snaking Ezra Blaine's .30-30 carbine from its boot as he did so. Swiftly he ground-tied the tired pony.

"Sounds like somebody target practisin',"

grunted the Phantom Sheriff, heading up the ledge which offered a route to the top of the cliffs. "It's a cinch it ain't no gun battle. The shots is too regularly spaced fer that."

The shots had ceased by the time Spook Sidlaw gained the level of the north rim. Then he halted stockstill, hands gripping his Winchester tensely at the scene before him.

Gila Jack Shadmer was standing spread-legged in front of his foam-flecked horse, only a few yards away.

In Shadmer's fists were a pair of Colt six-guns, from whose muzzles leaked twin plumes of white smoke. Thicker clouds of gun smoke had clotted the air about the Smoketree killer.

But it was not Gila Jack Shadmer who caught and held Spook Sidlaw's attention.

It was Joe Kurdle, his bullet-butchered corpse sagging over the pommel of Shadmer's saddle, blood trickling from a dozen wounds on the old miner's head and chest and abdomen.

Shadmer continued to stare at the body of the prospector he had sieved with .45 slugs, his eyes unblinking, his muscles as rigid as if he himself were a statue carved from granite.

And then a flash of sunlight on the barrel of Spook Sidlaw's rifle made Shadmer come to himself with a jerk, and whirl about to face the canyon rim.

Shadmer's red-rimmed eyes flared to show

the whites, as he stared at the crouched figure of the Phantom Sheriff, saw the waddy's thumb ear back the hammer of the .30-30 and lever a shell from magazine to breech.

"Looks like I got here too late to save Joe Kurdle," rasped Spook Sidlaw, stepping slowly forward. "But it's plain to see yuh chopped him to hash meat with yore smoke poles, Shadmer— an' him tied an' helpless."

Gila Jack Shadmer's arms dropped, still holding the smoking Colts. The bayed gambler seemed too frozen with horror and despair to answer.

"I'm countin' three, Shadmer!" said the Phantom Sheriff. "Then I'm goin' to shoot, an' shoot to kill. After the way you left me to die— an' after the way you butchered this pore old codger—I've decided yore carcass ain't worth haulin' back to Arizona on the hoof. So I'm givin' you yore chance to shoot it out with me, on an equal basis."

Gila Jack Shadmer swallowed hard. When his voice came, it was dead and hoarse, devoid of any defiance.

"I didn't kill Joe. His pump gave out an' he croaked nacheral. He cheated me—led me to a petered-out mine. I lost my head. I . . . I was triggerin' slugs into a dead man, Sidlaw."

The Phantom Sheriff cradled his gun butt against his shoulder, his eyes gleaming vengefully.

"It's showdown, Gila Jack. You ain't fit to draw another breath, an' most men would shoot yuh down like the dog yuh are. But I'm givin' yuh yore chance. Yuh got two hoglegs. I got this carbine. When I count three, fog them Colts!"

With a hoarse bellow of fear, Gila Jack Shadmer hurled his six-guns to the ground.

"They're empty, Sidlaw. Both of 'em. Yuh . . . yuh wouldn't shoot a unheeled man, would yuh?"

Sidlaw hesitated, anger making his nostrils flare.

"Stop yore whinin', Shadmer. I give yuh yore choice—either I handcuff yuh an' haul yuh back to Smoketree to hang legal—or else yuh shoot it out with me. I'll give yuh time to load yore guns."

Shadmer licked his lips in an agony of indecision. He had lost some of his fear now, and the stark horror in his eyes was replaced by a sinister glint."

"How do I know yuh won't plug me afore I kin reload?"

Sidlaw grounded his rifle stock impatiently.

"I ain't a murderer. If I'd wanted to kill yuh I could 'a' had it over with by now. Pick up them guns!"

Shadmer threw a glance over his shoulder. His beady eyes dropped to the ground, where his empty six-guns lay.

" 'Sta bueno, Sidlaw. You win. I'll put one ca'tridge in each Colt."

Shadmer stooped. Then, instead of scooping up the guns, he leaped suddenly to put Kurdle's horse between him and the Phantom Sheriff.

Running like a startled antelope, Gila Jack Shadmer bolted up the slope, heading for the brush-choked barranca which masked the entrance to the long-lost Spanish mine.

"Go ahead an' shoot, Sidlaw!" screamed the outlaw. "I ain't stretchin' no hangrope o' yourn!"

Sidlaw whipped the rifle stock to cheek, notched the sights on the fleeing crook's back.

Then he changed his mind, and set out in pursuit.

"I'll haul him back to Smoketree alive an' kickin'. I reckon I was loco even to think o' baitin' him into gunplay, in the first place!"

But Spook Sidlaw's high-heeled boots were ill adapted for running in the loose mine tailings. His strength had almost reached the limit. Twice he stumbled heavily, then picked himself up and slogged on in pursuit of the fleeing outlaw.

Gila Jack Shadmer, spurred by the hope of possible escape, smashed into the buckbrush and ignota which choked the mouth of the defile.

Momentarily checked by the wiry foliage, the outlaw flung a glance over his shoulder to see the Phantom Sheriff closing in the gap between

239

them, rifle held at arm's length, boots pumping hard over the rocks.

Frantically Gila Jack pushed his way on through the brush, the sound of Sidlaw's pursuit in his ears.

Reaching the clearing alongside the cliff walls, Shadmer glanced desperately about, hoping to find a club he could hurl at the grim lawman who was pounding through the brush behind him.

The black maw of the Spanish gold mine offered the only opportunity to forestall a showdown.

Blowing like a maverick calf, foam flecking his lips, Gila Jack Shadmer raced for the cavern mouth.

He flung himself into the dark hole in the rock, even as Spook Sidlaw fought his way clear of the chaparral and emerged into the open.

CHAPTER XXX.

Sidlaw fired a warning shot at the disappearing figure of the outlaw, but the lead flattened itself against the rocky wall of the Black Padre mine, even as Shadmer's scuttling legs vanished into the murky interior.

Sidlaw paused, lungs heaving painfully.

"Mebby I kin wait hyar until I starve him out—only that way I'd prob'ly starve myself first—"

Then the dismaying possibility that the gold mine might have an exit through which Shadmer could make his way to safety, caused the Phantom Sheriff to abandon the idea of standing guard outside the tunnel until he had rested up.

Rifle clutched grimly, the Phantom Sheriff stalked into the mouth of the tunnel.

Up ahead, he could hear Shadmer's tortured, animallike breathing as the outlaw scrambled madly into the pitch-blackness of the shaft.

Daylight filtered through the cavern mouth to show the lawman the rusty old coal-oil lantern which the prospectors had left hanging from a bracing timber.

"By gosh—if thar's any oil in that lantern, I kin use it!" panted Sidlaw, taking down the match and shaking it. Sloshing oil sounded inside the fuel tank.

Sidlaw took a match from his shirt pocket and

lighted the wick. The feeble glow of the lantern dispelled the dense blackness, showed him the mine tunnel curving up and away into the recesses of Furnace Mountain.

Even as his eyes focused down the cavern's throat, he saw Gila Jack Shadmer vanish around a far bend of the tunnel.

Sidlaw charged forward, lantern in one hand, rifle in the other. Now, with the lantern, he knew he would be safe from any chance of Shadmer lying in wait in the darkness to kill him with a chunk of quartz.

The sound of Shadmer's panic-stricken flight dinned against his eardrums, as the Phantom Sheriff gained the first elbow bend.

Moisture glinted from the cavern walls, reflecting the lantern's rays. The dust of Shadmer's passage hung in the humid atmosphere.

Here and there along the tunnel, Sidlaw could see hand-hewn timbers supporting the ceiling—timbers placed there, perhaps, by the ancient Spanish padres.

Sidlaw pushed on, disregarding the ominous pounding of his overtaxed heart.

"One thing—Shadmer ain't heeled. If I kin git him in sight, I'll put a slug in his foot to stop him. I can't take a chance o' that polecat findin' an exit an' makin' a gitaway, now that I practically got him captured."

The Phantom Sheriff paused from time to time as he worked his way along the twisting course of the shaft, to hear Shadmer's boots crunching slower and slower over the rubble, somewhere ahead.

Sidlaw felt like a hunter, tracking down a beast of prey. Sweat rained from his pores. His lungs ached. Ahead of him, his shadow waggled grotesquely on the rocky walls. The dungeonlike damp seemed to penetrate to his marrow, but he pushed on relentlessly, knowing that capture could not be far off.

Then he came to a triple fork in the mine, where the Spaniards had followed three gold veins in centuries past.

Finding which fork Shadmer had chosen was easy, due to the dust which smudged the atmosphere of the center tunnel.

"Shadmer! Yuh better halt up, if yuh want me to spare yore life!"

Sidlaw's voice was lost in clamoring echoes. He wondered if it was Shadmer's taunting laugh that wafted back down the wet-sided tunnel, or if it was his imagination.

The lantern rays cut a swath through the blackness as he rounded another bend in the tunnel. Gila Jack Shadmer was nowhere to be seen.

A dozen yards ahead, the tunnel was blocked by a yawning black abyss, where the diggings had struck a cleft in the subterranean rock structure.

For an instant, Sidlaw believed that Shadmer had plunged to his death in that pit. Then he saw a plank spanning the ten-foot gap, a plank that was still shaking from Shadmer's passage across it.

Evidently the reflected light of his lantern had saved Gila Jack from running blindly into the abyss, had picked out the board which the Kurdle brothers had probably put across the black gulf.

The mine tunnel turned at right angles, just beyond the chasm. Somewhere Sidlaw could hear trickling water. Then his ears caught the muffled, whistled breathing of his quarry, around the corner.

Sidlaw clutched his lantern handle and pushed forward toward the abyss.

The stuffiness of the air and the confusion of echoes told him that Shadmer had found dead end, up ahead. That being the case, showdown was near at hand.

Sidlaw reached the plank bridge, steadied its vibration with a boot toe. Then he started forward, treading as cautiously as a tight-rope walker.

His stomach knotted with suspense as he tried to keep his eyes from looking down into the pit. For all he knew, it might be hundreds of feet to the bottom of that fissure.

As he reached the center of the plank, holding

his arms wide for balance, Sidlaw heard the Smoketree gambler come back around the bend in the tunnel ahead.

He tore his eyes away from the precarious bridge, to see the leering outlaw snatch up a chunk of gold ore. Drawing back his arm, Gila Jack Shadmer measured the distance to the trapped sheriff, then hurled the quartz with all his strength.

"Go to blazes, Sidlaw—"

Frantically, Spook Sidlaw tried to swivel away from the speeding rock. It struck a glancing blow across his shoulder, destroying his balance, making his boots teeter sickeningly on the bouncing board underfoot.

A choked cry came from the Phantom Sheriff's lips as he felt the insecure plank slide away from under him.

He had a nightmarish vision of Gila Jack's triumphant visage, as he hurtled out into space.

Then he dropped from sight below the rim of the tunnel floor, the lantern in his clutches blowing out as he plummeted down into the black void of the underground chasm.

CHAPTER XXXI.

Gila Jack Shadmer crouched in the blackness for several minutes, his eyes retaining a mental image of the Phantom Sheriff in that awful moment when the lawman had teetered on the plank bridge, only to plummet from sight into the chasm which broke the floor of the gold mine.

The outlaw shuddered. Less than ten feet behind him the tunnel had ended in a sheer wall of stone, where the *conquistadores* had followed the gold-bearing vein until a fault ended it.

He had contemplated receiving a fatal bullet, once Spook Sidlaw captured him there. But now that was finished. Where his foe had dropped, Shadmer had no idea. There was no way of judging the depth of these subterranean cavities which miners encountered.

"Lucky fer me Sidlaw didn't kick that plank loose when he got hit by my rock," muttered the outlaw huskily, dropping to hands and knees and starting to crawl forward. "If he had, it'd 'a' meant finish fer me. I'd 'a' died like a trapped animal. That hole was too wide to jump!"

Inching forward, Gila Jack Shadmer groped exploring palms over the rocky floor until he came to the brink of the chasm. The blackness was so thick it seemed to press invisible fingers against his eyeballs, forcing them back into his head. No light penetrated this far into the Black Padre diggings.

His groping fingers found the plank bridge. He tested it for strength, then crawled out and straddled the board. He could not trust his sense of balance in crossing that perilous bridge over unknown gulfs of space.

Inch by inch he made his way across until he had reached the safety of the opposite ledge.

He cupped a hand behind his ear, listening intently for signs of what had happened to Spook Sidlaw.

Then he picked up a small rock and dropped it into the chasm. To his surprise it struck bottom very soon, indicating a shallow drop.

Water drained and gurgled somewhere down inside the mountain. He could hear his dropped stone clattering off down into the chasm. It was still rolling when the echoes died out.

"Sidlaw prob'ly spilled a mile," chuckled Shadmer, getting to his feet and groping his way out of the mine tunnel. "I reckon all o' the meat's been rubbed offn his skeleton by now."

Five minutes after Shadmer's departure, a match scratched down in the abyss.

By its feeble glow, the Phantom Sheriff took stock of his situation.

He had fallen about eight feet, his drop

cushioned by a cone-shaped heap of rock chips and sand. Then he had apparently skidded a few yards before his sprawling body came to a halt. Dust still hung thickly in the air.

Heavy chaps had again saved his legs from severe cuts or bruises, and the steep slant of the debris pile—formed of rock chips from the mine tunnel—had accounted for the cushioning effect of his fall.

"Lucky I was able to keep from groanin' or breathin' noisy when Shadmer was shinnyin' acrost that plank up thar," thought Sidlaw as the match went out between his fingers. "Otherwise he'd have heaved rocks down hyar till he was shore I was out o' the way fer keeps."

Scratching another match, Sidlaw spotted his lantern, blown out during the brief fall through dank, chilly space. Its glass chimney was shattered, but when he ignited the wick he was rewarded by a feeble flame which dispelled the awesome gloom.

"Gosh—I'm lucky this wasn't a hundred-foot drop—or am I?"

Merciful death might have been preferable to the unknown fate that awaited him, now that he had a chance to look about. The cavity in the earth which the ancient Spanish miners had tapped with their mine tunnel, was formed of beetling rock walls slick as glass, affording no chance to climb out.

The guttering rays of the lantern wick picked out his fallen .30-30. The Winchester's walnut stock had cracked on impact, but a quick inspection told him that the firing mechanism was intact and that the barrel had not been damaged by the fall.

Gradually, as his eyes accustomed themselves to the pale-orange glow of the wick, Sidlaw made out the other details of the pitfall into which he had plunged.

The debris pile onto which he had fallen was unmistakably the rock which had been chiseled and shoveled out of the tunnel above. Without it, he realized sure death would have been his.

The ends of the fissure vanished beyond the range of his light. Guttering water, somewhere back in the throat of the darkness to his right, assured him that he would not perish of thirst, at any rate.

"If I'm goin' to git out o' here, I got to hurry," groaned Sidlaw, picking up the broken lantern and his rifle, and starting to scramble up the debris pile toward its summit. "Because Gila Jack has lit a shuck out o' hyar. From what he said, the Kurdle twins had finished working out the old mine, so there was nothing to keep Shadmer here."

That being the case, the Smoketree killer would undoubtedly appropriate Sidlaw's provisions and horse, untie Kurdle's corpse from his own mount and continue his flight toward some Mexican settlement which had been his original destination.

Afoot and without food here in the bleak malpais, Sidlaw realized that even if he succeeded in getting out of the Black Padre alive, he would never be able to reach Arizona before his endurance gave out completely.

He climbed to the peak of the cone-shaped pile of debris which had been dumped from the tunnel above.

Eight feet above the debris pile he could see the plank which had served as a bridge for Joe and Jake Kurdle to cross the fissure.

"Might as well be eighty feet," groaned the cowboy as he reached upward. "I cain't touch the plank, an' this rock is too loose fer me to do any jumpin'."

As it was his own six feet of height, plus the added length of his arms, made it impossible for him to reach the plank overhead; for each time he stretched his fingertips toward the board, his boots wedged deeper into the soft rock formation.

Then an idea came. He tossed the .30-30 up on the rim of the tunnel floor, to be rid of it, and peeled off his red-checkered shirt.

Into one sleeve he tied a jackknife to weight it. Then, gripping the shirt by the left sleeve, Sidlaw tossed the shirt up and over the plank above him so that the other sleeve with the weighted cuff dropped over the plank and hung from the opposite side.

Even as he gripped the two sleeves of the shirt and tested his weight on the sturdy fabric, the lantern stuck in the dirt underfoot guttered, flickered, and went out, its fuel supply exhausted.

Sidlaw shuddered at the tomblike blackness which closed in. But the reassuring tug of the shirt which he had looped over the plank kept panic from rising within him.

Twisting the sleeves together in a wringing motion until they formed a rope, Spook Sidlaw started climbing. The strong fabric supported his weight as he went upward and hooked strong-muscled fingers over the edge of the plank.

The plank itself bowed under his weight, but a moment later he had chinned himself over the edge and was hauling his knees safely to the top of the board. Shakily he redonned the shirt.

It was but the matter of seconds to crawl on hands and knees to the safety of the tunnel ledge. His groping hands found the rifle he had thrown up, and then he got to his feet.

"Whew! Gettin' out o' that mess makes me feel plumb *bueno* again!" he muttered.

He found the wall of the tunnel and followed it back to the triple forks which joined the main cavern.

He stopped to listen, but he was positive that

251

Gila Jack Shadmer was no longer inside the Black Padre. The outlaw's first reaction would be like his own—a desire to get out of this coal-black cave as soon as possible.

Realizing that the sound of his footsteps would be magnified, Sidlaw conquered his impulse to run, and groped his way along the twisting course of the gold mine until his eyes caught sight of welcome daylight streaming through the mouth of the tunnel.

He waited until his eyes were accustomed to the brilliant light, then worked his way to the mouth of the Black Padre.

Shadmer's boot tracks led out into the brush. Peering cautiously about as he left the tunnel behind him, the Phantom Sheriff made his way toward the buck brush.

With infinite caution, he crawled through the undergrowth, shoving his broken-stocked .30-30 before him.

Then, reaching the outer fringe of chaparral, Spook Sidlaw grinned with triumph.

Gila Jack Shadmer was sitting on a boulder midway down the slope, devouring the parched corn which had been part of Sidlaw's meager food supplies.

The outlaw had untied Joe Kurdle's bullet-riddled frame from his mount and had flung it callously aside. Already buzzards were wheeling up in the blue, awaiting the departure of the men so that they could feast on the dead prospector's remains.

The two horses flung up their heads, scenting the approach of another human. But Gila Jack Shadmer was too busy resting and eating to notice the stealthy advance of the Phantom Sheriff, tiptoeing down the slope with rifle held in readiness for emergency.

Gila Jack Shadmer's holsters contained his guns once more, and Sidlaw knew they would be loaded now.

The rattle of a dislodged stone under the sheriff's boot sole caused Shadmer to jerk erect, staring about him in the direction of Bitter River's gorge.

"Reach fer a cloud, Shadmer. I'm sort o' hopin' yuh'll try an' run for it ag'in this time, because I don't think we got enough grub to last the two of us back to the border."

Shadmer stood up, hands poised over gun butts as he heard the familiar voice behind him.

Moving with the jerky wooden motions of a puppet on wires, Gila Jack Shadmer turned around, eyes blazing with hatred and despair as he saw the Phantom Sheriff squinting at him down the barrel of a Winchester.

At last he found his voice.

"Yuh . . . yuh ain't human, Sidlaw. How kin I buck a phantom?"

With the words he had hoped would throw his

enemy off guard, Gila Jack Shadmer stabbed for his guns.

The rifle in Sidlaw's grasp bucked and roared, and the soft-nosed slug sliced flesh from the muscle on Shadmer's left forearm.

Spun about and dumped off his feet by the impact of the bullet, Shadmer sprawled headlong as the Phantom Sheriff pounced like a cougar and whipped his Colt .45s from the killer's grasp.

"I found out I wasn't the stripe to murder yuh, after all, Shadmer!" panted the sheriff coolly, as he notched his handcuffs over the outlaw's hairy wrists. "Stand up. We're headin' back to Smoketree, soon as I kin give Joe Kurdle a decent burial."

CHAPTER XXXII.

It was three days before Spook Sidlaw rode once more down Smoketree's main street, leading a horse, astride which sat Gila Jack Shadmer, handcuffed with the fetters which Sheriff Buck Clawson had long wished to put on Shadmer's wrists.

Men, viewing the two riders from saloon porch chairs, failed to recognize either of them. Like gaunt scarecrows they sat their horses, ravaged by thirst and hunger, covered with trail dust, riding horses which had nearly reached the limit of their endurance.

Doc Frazer scrambled out of his office as the two bedraggled riders drew rein at his hitch bar. A glad cry came from the old coroner's throat as he recognized Sidlaw by the dusty golden star pinned to his shirt.

"Yuh look like a ghost comin' out o' hell, with the devil himself fer a prisoner, Spook!" cried the cow-town doctor as Sidlaw shook hands. "Son, yuh've aged ten years since that locomotive wreck. But I see yuh brung back yore man."

Sidlaw lifted his gaze above the false-fronted adobe shacks to stare at Marie Clawson's cottage up on Mescal Hill. The sight seemed to revive his flagging spirits.

"Let's stow Shadmer in the calaboose," said the Phantom Sheriff wearily, as he assisted his prisoner down off his horse. "We're both about dead, I reckon. I'll tell yuh what happened, soon as I git some grub in my belly."

Flanked on either side by Sidlaw and Frazer, the captured gun boss of Smoketree staggered toward the jail building, head slumped on his chest. No longer was he the swaggering, gaudily dressed card sharper of old.

"Every cell in the place is full, Spook," said Frazer as they reached the jail house. "Rustlers from the Lazy Diamond that we captured the other day at Gunbore Tunnel, yuh know. They'd tear Shadmer apart if you put him in thar with 'em—on account o' him desertin' his men the way he did."

Sidlaw led his fatigued prisoner into Buck Clawson's office. Then he jerked to attention, as if he had just heard Frazer's words.

"Huh? The jail's full? But we got to stow him somewhar so that his saloon *companeros* won't try to rescue him, doc."

The grizzled old coroner pointed out the window toward the courthouse nearby.

"See that annex on the back end o' the courthouse?" asked Frazer. "The stone-walled addition that butts up agin' the main buildin'? That's the old Malpais County jail, afore we built this one. Yuh'll find keys to it in Buck's desk thar. They use it fer a storeroom now, but I reckon it'll hold Gila Jack."

Thus it was that Gila Jack Shadmer was taken away from the main jail, filled with vengeful rustlers thirsting for Shadmer's life, and locked up in the one-story jail room behind the courthouse.

"I got a legal right to talk to a lawyer, ain't I?" whined Shadmer when Sidlaw clanged the barred door shut and locked it with Buck Clawson's key.

Sidlaw shrugged wearily.

"Reckon so. But is thar a law hombre in Malpais County who'd have the gall to plead a case fer a snake like you?"

Shadmer nodded, crafty lights kindling in his gaunt eyes.

"Curly Bardoo was a lawyer onct. I want to see him."

Sidlaw glanced at Frazer, scowling.

"Bardoo? Yuh mean the bartender at the Lucky Dollars—the busky who brought word to Francisco Yuma's smugglin' meetin' that Smoketree was up in arms agin' you?"

"The same," Shadmer said huskily. "Any objections to me seein' Bardoo about defendin' me at my trial?"

Sidlaw nodded after a moment's hesitation.

"Reckon not. But it'll take a lot more'n a stove-up whiskey-slinger to talk you out o' stretchin' rope, Shadmer," the Phantom Sheriff said, as he and Frazer headed for the side-door. "I'll send him over, soon as I've rested up. Frazer, you better roust up Sammy Duncan an' have him stand guard over Shadmer. We ain't takin' no chances—until we got him in boothill an' the clods tamped down."

Locking the courthouse annex, Sidlaw handed the ring of keys to Frazer for the coroner to turn over to Deputy Sheriff Sammy Duncan.

"You better rattle yore hocks over to my spare bedroom an' git some shut-eye, son," advised the medico as they headed across the courthouse yard toward the main jail. "You look like yuh been drawed through a knothole. What in blazes happened since you headed out after Shadmer, anyhow?"

The Phantom Sheriff heaved a deep sigh of weariness.

"It's a long story, doc. It involves the lost Black Padre Mine, an' two murdered prospectors, an' trackin'—"

Sidlaw was interrupted by the sound of running footsteps. As he and the doctor halted, they recognized Sammy Duncan, the deputy sheriff, sprinting toward them from the main street.

Lumbering along behind the young deputy was Curly Bardoo, Shadmer's bartender at the Lucky Dollars.

"Howdy, Spook!" panted Duncan, gripping the waddy's hand in warm greeting. "Jumpin'

258

juniper, but I'm glad to see yuh back! I hear yuh dabbed yore twine on Shadmer."

"Yeah!" puffed Curly Bardoo, swabbing his perspiring jowls with a corner of his saloon apron. "Is that right, Sidlaw? You got my boss in jail yonder?"

The Phantom Sheriff nodded.

"That's right, Bardoo. Here, Sammy—take these keys. Gila Jack wants to make *habla* with Bardoo here—claims Bardoo used to be a lawyer. Step over hyar, Bardoo, an' let me frisk yuh."

Bardoo glowered as the Phantom Sheriff deprived him of a sleeve-hidden derringer, a knife secreted in a bootleg sheath, and his thonged-down Colt .45.

"Call fer these playthings at the sheriff's office after you're done palaverin' with Gila Jack," said the sheriff. "Sammy, you stay in the jail room until Bardoo leaves. An' another thing—git Slats Waterbury to help guard that jail, come dark. We cain't take any chances o' that saloon gang tryin' to pull a jail break fer Shadmer. Soon as I've got some sleep, I'll jine yuh."

Duncan grinned, realizing that the Phantom Sheriff had given his orders in Bardoo's hearing for a very evident purpose.

The Phantom Sheriff departed for Frazer's house. In his present condition he did not want to call on Marie Clawson and report to her the good news that his mission in Smoketree was finished, that he could now return her brother's gold star and feel free to drift on his way.

Somehow, Spook Sidlaw of Wyoming had lost the wanderlust which had made him a restless, roving tumbleweed for so many years. But he could not admit this to Marie Clawson.

CHAPTER XXXIII.

Sammy Duncan unlocked the courthouse annex and permitted Curly Bardoo to step inside to interview his boss, Gila Jack Shadmer. He remained on guard at the doorway while the bartender and the prisoner went into a whispered conference.

"Break it up, boys!" snarled Duncan. "If you got any *habla* fer Bardoo to hear, Gila Jack, speak yore piece out loud!"

Gila Jack Shadmer winked at Bardoo as the latter prepared to leave.

"*Bueno*, chief," grunted the barkeep. "I'll go over to Willie Wong's place an' buy yuh a good meal. It's hard tellin' when the county'd git around to feedin' yuh."

Sammy Duncan eyed Bardoo suspiciously as the latter left the jail room. There was a crafty glitter in Bardoo's buckshot eyes which the deputy sheriff didn't like.

"Don't plan any shenanigans tonight, Bardoo!" warned the deputy as he relocked the door. "When yuh got Shadmer's grub at the chink's, I'll take it in to him. An' thar'll be a triple guard on duty hyar all night, an' all the time till the trial."

Bardoo leered.

"I'm jest goin' to consult my law books an' see ifn I kin figger out a way to keep the chief from doin' a air jig," he said. "But I reckon Shadmer killin' that Chinaman, Willie Wong, when he got that engine to rollin' out o' Gunbore Tunnel—I reckon that killin' alone will swing the boss."

In spite of his pessimistic outlook regarding his new client, Bardoo's eyes were optimistic as he headed for his quarters in the upper story of the saloon. He had listened hard to the brief orders which Gila Jack Shadmer had given him in the jail cell, and now he was going about putting those orders into operation.

Shadmer had had plenty of time to scheme and plan during his trip back from the Black Padre Mine down in Mexico. And Curly Bardoo was forced to admit that Gila Jack's chances of beating the noose were very good—though not through any legal route.

Going upstairs to his room, Curly Bardoo proceeded to pack a pair of Gila Jack's saddlebags with provisions. Into them went a thick sheaf of greenbacks, part of the cash which Shadmer kept hidden for emergency use. The money was followed by foodstuffs—dried meat, coffee, salt, sugar, flapjack dough.

Next Bardoo carried the saddlebags down to Shadmer's private office and got the outlaw's pair of stubby-barreled Colt .32s—small guns which Shadmer carried in shoulder holsters when he was gambling.

Next on his list of duties was ordering Shadmer's supper. A saloon helper was ordered to go over to Willie Wong's All-American Cafe—now managed by the Chinaman's half-Indian widow—and buy a meal to take over to Willie Wong's murderer.

Bardoo then went back to his bartending duties, working as placidly as if nothing unusual were astir. He worked until darkness had enveloped the town and the saloon business was beginning to get brisk. Then he turned the bar over to an assistant and retired to the privacy of Gila Jack's quarters. He pocketed Shadmer's Colt .32s.

Shouldering the saddlebags, he paused long enough to rummage through Shadmer's box of fishing tackle and took out a spool of strong silk fishing line. Pocketing it, he headed out a back door and went out to the saloon's private stable.

From a row of horses he selected the fastest bronc bearing the Lazy Diamond iron and saddled it up. Behind the cantle he buckled the saddlebags, stuffed with supplies.

"Reckon this'll see the chief safe into Mexico before midnight," chuckled Bardoo. "An' I reckon that'll be the last that Smoketree will ever see o' Gila Jack. His luck's played out hyar."

Bardoo hitched the horse which he had prepared for flight to the corral gate. Then he

263

walked down a dark side street toward the long-abandoned Green Goose dance hall, which was owned by Shadmer.

Unlocking the deserted building with one of Shadmer's keys, Bardoo entered the barnlike structure and climbed a ladder to the attic. A window in the gable opened on the wide porch which flanked the dance hall.

Peering out of the glassless window, Curly Bardoo could look down into the back yard of the courthouse. Not fifty feet away was the rear of the jail annex.

A sickle-shaped moon rode the Arizona heavens, and by its light Bardoo could see several things. The wide steel-barred window of Gila Jack's cell; the figure of Deputy Sheriff Sammy Duncan, smoking a cigarette on the doorstep of the jail, and the figure of Slats Waterbury, who was marching along the wooden fence of the courthouse yard, so close that Bardoo could recognize the tune Waterbury was humming as he passed the front of the dance hall.

Waterbury was shouldering a double-barreled shotgun. Duncan had assigned him the job of patrolling the back yard, to warn him of any attempt on the part of Shadmer's henchmen to sneak up to the jail and saw out the window bars.

The overhanging eaves of the dance hall threw the porch roof in dense shadow. Curly Bardoo straddled out the window and reached in his pocket for the reel of fishing line.

He tied the line around a heavy pocketknife which he carried. Then, waiting until Slats Waterbury had marched to the far end of the courthouse yard, he gave the low call of a hoot owl.

Almost instantly a match flared inside the jail window and Bardoo saw Gila Jack Shadmer lighting a quirly. It was the signal that the jailed outlaw had heard the owl hoot and was ready.

"Now to see how straight my aim is," grunted Bardoo. "I used to be able to split a ace o' hearts with a knife at fifty feet—so slinging a closed jackknife into that window ought to be easy."

Grasping the end of the coiled fishing line in one hand and the jackknife in the other, Curly Bardoo wound up then hurled the knife in a wide arc through space.

The knife sped toward the big target offered by the jail window. In its flight the thrown knife unreeled the coiled silken fishing line behind it.

There was a muffled thud from inside the jail cell as Shadmer caught Bardoo's expertly thrown knife in a spread-out blanket.

"*Muy bien*!" Bardoo felt the fishing line go taut as Shadmer pulled it from inside the jail. When the slack was taken up, Curly Bardoo made his end of the silken cord secure to a nail stuck in the clapboards of the dance hall.

Waterbury, the trudging shotgun guard, passed

by once more on his monotonous rounds, little dreaming that a spider web of strong silk stretched at a steep angle from the dance-hall building across the fence, over his head and down into the jail window.

While Waterbury was making his return circuit of the board fence, Bardoo untied the fishing line and threaded the end of it through the trigger guards of the two short-barreled Colts he had carried over from the saloon.

Again he waited until Waterbury was at the farthest point in his march. A faint jerk on the line by Shadmer indicated that the outlaw chief was ready.

Bardoo gave the first six-gun a shove. Gravity carried it swiftly and noiselessly down the steep incline of the fishing line strung taut between jail window and dance hall.

Waiting tensely at his cell window, Gila Jack Shadmer's outstretched hand closed over the gun as it skidded home, preventing any betraying clang of metal against window bars.

He yanked the fishing line once more, and a few seconds later, with a soft hissing sound, the second Colt .32 coasted down the line into his waiting hand.

Shadmer pocketed the stubby-barreled guns, cut the stout silk cord. The sagging end of the string was Bardoo's signal to haul the line in, its usefulness at an end.

By the time Slats Waterbury had marched back alongside the jail, Bardoo was straddling back inside the dance-hall window across the street, his work finished.

Things were quiet in Smoketree during the next half-hour—deceptively quiet. It was somehow like the lull before a storm.

Then the hard adobe ruts of the main street resounded to the clatter of Sammy Duncan's cow boots as the young deputy sheriff raced from the courthouse to the lamplighted home of Dr. Frazer.

Slamming open the coroner's door without the formality of a knock, Duncan surprised Frazer in his kitchen, busy preparing a meal. Helping him was Marie Clawson, her buckskin riding skirt and blouse hidden by a housewife's gingham apron.

"Whar's Spook?" cried Duncan, his eyes glaring wildly.

The sheriff's daughter put a finger to her lips and gestured toward a bedroom door opening off the parlor.

"Been sound asleep ever since he rode into town—never even told me hello!" she pouted with mock chagrin. "What's the matter, Sammy?"

Duncan spun on his heel and headed toward Sidlaw's door.

"Matter? All hell's busted loose, that's all! Gila Jack Shadmer's gone an' killed himself!"

CHAPTER XXXIV.

The Phantom Sheriff opened his eyes and blinked against the glare of a coal-oil lamp carried into the darkened bedroom by Marie Clawson. He had been wakened from his sleep of exhaustion by the frantic shaking of Sammy Duncan.

"Howdy—Marie!" He grinned sheepishly, swinging his legs off the bed and rubbing his eyes hard. "I . . . I figgered to spruce myself up afore yuh saw me—"

"Listen, Spook!" cried the deputy sheriff. "Thar's hell to pay! Gila Jack Shadmer committed suicide—hung himself with his belt to a window bar! I jest discovered it!"

Sidlaw blinked, wide awake now. "He—*what?*"

"Hung himself. I heard a gaggin' sound, an' I unlocks the door an' rushes in to investigate. Lit a lantern—an' thar he was, strangled to death. He cheated us out o' hangin' him!"

Sidlaw yanked his battered Stetson off a bedpost and clapped it on his head. Then he hitched his shell belts into position.

"Did yuh cut him down?" he asked the deputy,

"No!" exploded Duncan. "I didn't even unlock the cell."

Sidlaw turned swiftly to Marie Clawson.

"Sammy'll wait here with you, Marie," he

said brusquely. "Doc an' me will go over an' investigate."

Dr. Frazer snatched up his emergency kit and followed Spook Sidlaw out into the night, bound for the courthouse jail.

No sound greeted the pair as they unlocked the side door of the rockwalled annex to the courthouse and rushed inside.

The light of the lantern Duncan had lighted showed Gila Jack Shadmer hanging limply from his pants belt, which had been looped about his neck and buckled to a bar of the window. His knees were bent, his boots touching the floor.

"His neck ain't broke, but a man kin strangle almost instantly that way," grunted Dr. Frazer professionally, as the Phantom Sheriff unlocked the cell door with feverish haste. "But we'll see if he's got a spark o' life left in his mangy carcass—"

Sidlaw stared at the outlaw's purpled face. Shadmer's tongue protruded from his lips, but the eyes were screwed shut instead of popping outward as Sidlaw had expected.

Frazer supported Shadmer's body with one arm as he lifted his weight and jerked the leather noose from under the man's jaw.

"Look out, doc—it's a trick—"

Even as Spook shouted the warning an amazing change took place in the supposed suicide.

Gila Jack Shadmer brought his hands from

behind his back to reveal two stubby-barreled Colt .32s.

Dr. Frazer wilted as one Colt muzzle thudded against his chin. The Phantom Sheriff felt his own six-gun snag its front sight in his holster as he tried to duck Gila Jack Shadmer's vicious charge.

The killer's other .32 zipped upward in a short arc that ended with a cracking sound across Spook Sidlaw's ear. Then blackness wiped out the sneeringly triumphant face of the outlaw as the Phantom Sheriff sagged on the jail floor.

Shadmer stood panting heavily, sweat dripping from his skin as he stared down at the limp bodies of his victims.

His ruse had worked perfectly. The fake suicide had made Deputy Sheriff Sammy Duncan bring Sidlaw and Frazer to the jail and open his cell. Slats Waterbury, the shotgun guard, was still patrolling the back yard, in ignorance of what was transpiring inside the jail annex.

Shadmer worked swiftly and according to carefully laid plans. Leaving the cell, he locked the grated door and pocketed the key ring, thereby imprisoning the two stunned men in the cell.

Then his beady eyes came to rest on the tier of kerosene cans which he had noticed stacked against the wall next to the courthouse proper.

Since the building of the new Malpais County jail, earlier in Buck Clawson's administration, the annex had served as a woodshed and storeroom for the courthouse. The five-gallon cans of coal oil were for fueling the lamps in the courtroom and county offices.

"I got to leave Smoketree anyhow—so I might as well hand out the kind o' revenge them skunks deserve," grated Gila Jack Shadmer, heading across the room. "I reckon I got plenty o' time to work in. I didn't have to fire any shots to rouse Waterbury out thar—"

Shadmer opened the door entering the rear of the courtroom by means of a key in the sheriff's ring. He carried several cans of kerosene into the corridor and dumped their contents over the floor and walls.

The last can of oil he poured on the granite floor of the stone jail room, splashing it on cords of stacked-up firewood.

Then, jerking out a handkerchief, the outlaw spread it on the floor just inside the hallway threshhold and made sure one corner of it touched the puddle of oil. The opposite corner of the handkerchief Shadmer ignited with a match.

The cloth started smoldering, fire eating across the cotton fabric. In less than half a minute Shadmer knew the improvised fuse would touch off the spilled oil.

That done, Shadmer cast a final glance at the

figures of Dr. Frazer and the Phantom Sheriff, locked helpless inside the cell.

Then Shadmer headed for the outside door, shut and locked it, and raced across the courthouse yard toward the back street that flanked his private stable behind the Lucky Dollars Saloon. If Bardoo had carried out his orders there would be a fast pony hitched to the corral with saddlebags loaded for a getaway.

Hardly had Shadmer gained the back street when he heard a muffled *whooosh* behind him. He flung a glance over his shoulder and saw the courthouse windows glowing with rosy color as flames leaped inside the building.

Then he ran at top speed for his stable a block away.

Over in Dr. Frazer's shack on the main street, Marie Clawson and Sammy Duncan were standing on the doorstep, talking earnestly.

"It isn't like Gila Jack to kill himself, Sammy!" the girl was protesting. "Something's fishy. I wish you hadn't left the jail until you were dead sure he—Sammy! *Look!*"

Duncan whirled to follow the direction of Marie's pointing arm. He was in time to see the windows of the Malpais County courthouse leap into form as rose-pink rectangles. Behind the windows, cherry flames danced and flickered.

Duncan stared aghast for a moment, then he cried hoarsely: "The courthouse is afire!"

Without another word he rushed out into the street and headed for the burning building, the girl at his heels.

Slats Waterbury, the shotgun deputy who had been patrolling the back yard, vaulted the board fence and ran up to Duncan as they reached the side door of the jail.

"What's happened?" yelled Waterbury frantically. "When I smelled smoke I run to the jail winder an' looked in—an' instead o' Gila Jack bein' in that cell, it's the Phantom Sheriff an' Doc Frazer. Both of 'em sprawled on the cell floor—"

Sammy Duncan wrenched hard on the jail doorknob.

"Locked!" he groaned, his face going white. "Shadmer was bluffin'. He's knocked out doc an' Spook an' locked 'em inside to burn!"

CHAPTER XXXV.

Marie Clawson didn't wait to see the desperate onslaught which Sammy Duncan and Slats Waterbury made with their shoulders against the thick oak planks of the jail door.

She knew too well the impossibility of breaking the lock or the door, and she knew there was no other way into the stone-walled jail, what with the corridor door blocked by fire.

Instead, the sheriff's daughter sped to her dead father's office on the main street, flung open the door and dropped on her knees alongside Buck Clawson's ancient safe.

Marie, having acted as her father's helper in business and bookkeeping matters during his terms as sheriff, possessed the combination to the rusty old strong box.

She spun the nickeled dial with steady fingers, swung open the vault door and rummaged in a drawer for a duplicate ring of keys to the courthouse, jail, and other Malpais County property in Smoketree.

"I mustn't be too late!" she breathed in a desperate whisper.

Smoketree citizens were heading for the burning building from all directions, on foot and on horseback. Flames were leaping from all six windows on the south wall of the courthouse as Marie Clawson crossed the weed-grown yard, the big ring of keys jangling in her hand.

A wall of searing heat struck her as she reached the jail door and hunted desperately for the proper key.

No one except Sammy Duncan and Waterbury knew of the helpless prisoners in the unused jail at the back end of the courthouse; and they had fled to a nearby blacksmith shop to get hacksaws with which to make a hopeless attempt at sawing out the window bars.

Men were congregating at the front end of the doomed building, to help save county records and other property.

Marie Clawson's shaking fingers managed to unlock the jail door. Smoke and flame-hot air smote her face as she headed blindly through the murk for the cells.

As yet the fire had not reached the kerosene, which made the rock floor slippery underfoot. The roar of the conflagration in the courthouse proper dinned in her ears as she reached the grated door of the cell.

Through smoke-seared eyes the girl caught sight of Spook Sidlaw rearing to his feet inside the cell, clutching the iron bars. Dr. Frazer was stirring on the cell floor, blood running from a bruise on his jaw.

"Hurry . . . Marie . . . before . . . that oil

catches—" the Phantom Sheriff said huskily. "Doc . . . can't walk! We'll have to lug him—"

His words didn't reach the girl over the deafening crackle of the blaze which was converting the courtroom into an inferno.

Precious seconds ticked by while Marie tried key after key. Even as she found the proper one, a muffled explosion knocked her sharply against the bars.

With an angry bellow, the kerosene which had drenched the jail's floor and woodpile burst into lurid flame, ignited by showering sparks carried into the annex by the draft from the blazing hallway.

The sheer heat of the explosion made the Phantom Sheriff recoil inside the jail, arm uplifted to shield his face as he grabbed Dr. Frazer and boosted the oldster's limp frame over one powerful shoulder.

"We're . . . done for . . . Marie!" choked Sidlaw, as he came outside the cell and seized the girl's arm. "We'll never make it . . . to that door . . . through the fire!"

Marie Clawson snatched a threadbare blanket from the prison cot and flung it over Dr. Frazer's snowy head to protect him from the licking flames. Yet she realized they couldn't possibly get through that living bank of fire to the safety of the outer doorway without all three of them being overcome.

"Keep behind me!" she screamed in Sidlaw's ear. "We can get out . . . through attic—"

Marie Clawson had spent her girlhood around the courthouse which had been her father's headquarters during the past ten years. She was thoroughly familiar with the building, and had often played hide-and-seek up in the attic of the jail.

Now she headed for the wall ladder opposite the flame which was devouring the stored wood and kindling next to the doorway. Spook Sidlaw staggered after her, shouldering Frazer's inert form.

How they ever got up the ladder to the opening in the jail ceiling, Sidlaw never knew.

The attic was like an oven from the heat below, but they were no longer in immediate danger.

"This way—ventilator in the gable!" cried Marie Clawson, crawling through smoke-clouded murk toward the end of the annex. "Not a long drop—it's the only chance—"

Bumping their heads against low rafters, crawling through inch-thick dust and tangled spider webs, the pair dragged Dr. Frazer to the ventilator, an opening covered with crisscrossed laths.

Clawing desperately at the latticework, the Phantom Sheriff ripped the laths aside, sucking in the sweet, cool air which whistled through the opening.

The ground was twelve feet below. They managed to get Dr. Frazer's body out of the ventilator opening, lowered him to arm's length, then dropped him the remaining six feet.

"You next, Marie. Don't reckon I'll ever forget the grit an' courage you showed in savin' us tonight—"

The girl crawled out, clung to Sidlaw's hands until she could kick herself away from the stone wall and drop.

The cowboy sheriff hung from the ventilator sill with his fingers and plummeted ground-ward to land heavily in the weeds. He got up and lurched over to pick up Dr. Frazer again.

"We better git doc away—get him home," panted Sidlaw. "It's too hot to take the short cut. We'll use that back gate."

They made their way across the rear yard, opened a gate in the high board fence adjoining the alley next to the Green Goose dance hall. Behind them the courthouse roof was sagging as fire ate into the rafters with a greedy roar.

Thudding hoofbeats made the two stare up the alley, expecting to see Sammy Duncan arriving with hacksaws.

Instead, Marie Clawson screamed with horror as they saw Gila Jack Shadmer rein up alongside them, the firelight over the board fence painting his haggard features with scarlet.

Shadmer drew a six-gun with blinding speed and pulled trigger.

The Phantom Sheriff felt the numbing shock of the bullet which drove him back against the fence. Then he dropped, with Dr. Frazer's body sprawling on top of him.

Marie Clawson jumped to his side with a low cry of grief. Even as she did so Gila Jack Shadmer leaned from the saddle to scoop an iron-muscled arm about the girl's waist.

Before she knew what had happened, the escaping outlaw had pulled her to the pommel, holding her with a tight elbow as he roweled his bronc into a full gallop.

Thundering at top speed down the alley behind Shadmer came Curly Bardoo, who had elected to throw his lot in with his chief's in some refuge below the border.

"A posse'll think twice afore they shoot at Bardoo or me," snarled Gila Jack in Marie's ear, "if we're carryin' you, gal!"

They left the alley and sped toward the cactus-dotted expanse of Whispering Desert, hauntingly spectral in the rays of the crescent moon.

CHAPTER XXXVI.

Bardoo reined up in a flurry of dust as he saw the Phantom Sheriff reel to his feet, both hands squeezing a blood-drenched bullet wound on his right leg. "Eat lead, yuh danged tin-star—"

Spook Sidlaw swiveled a holster for a hip shot at point-blank range. Even as Curly Bardoo's six-gun leaped from leather, a spurt of orange flame stabbed from the tip of Sidlaw's holster.

With a gagging sound Curly Bardoo reared backward in his saddle, a bullet hole leaking crimson over his heart.

Sick with pain, the Phantom Sheriff staggered out to haul the dead bartender from the stirrups. Wrenching the bridle reins from Bardoo's clutching fingers, Sidlaw climbed into the saddle and clutched the saddlehorn for support as Bardoo's horse fled in panicked flight.

The bite of cool desert wind cleared Sidlaw's throbbing head somewhat as the huts of the Mexican quarter blurred past.

Mushrooming smoke rose in a lurid column above the doomed courthouse behind him as Sidlaw clung frantically to the horse.

Light from the demon-rind moon illuminated a zigzag path of settling dust, indicating to Sidlaw the course Gila Jack Shadmer had taken in his kidnap dash into the waste lands.

Spurring for the utmost speed Bardoo's horse was capable of, the Phantom Sheriff followed the dusty trail through the brush, doggedly clinging to consciousness as he rode.

Moonlight showed him a flying black dot on the desert below him as he sped at full gallop along a cactus-spiny ridge. Sidlaw reined to the southward, following the rim of a dry coulee which he knew would intersect Shadmer's line of flight.

His wounded leg no longer tortured him. Instead it was a dead, numb weight tugging at his body.

Two miles behind him, now, the horizon wore a peach-colored glow. Billowing red flames were visible occasionally above the acres of chaparral as the courthouse room sprouted naked fire.

Then, sweeping like a comet out into a clearing, Spook Sidlaw caught a glimpse of Gila Jack Shadmer riding hard less than a hundred yards to the east and north of him.

The outlaw's bronc was traveling slower than his own, due to the added weight of the struggling girl flung across his pommel.

By the time Sidlaw had closed the gap by half, Shadmer suddenly drew rein. With a start, Sidlaw recognized the spot as the rock-carpeted slope where Shadmer had ambushed Freddie Clawson, and where the dying Texan had given Sidlaw the gold star of the Phantom Sheriff—the badge which was pinned even now to the front of Sidlaw's shirt.

"Hurry up, Bardoo!" came Shadmer's yell out of the wind. "Is anybody trailin' us?"

And then, even as the Phantom Sheriff galloped recklessly down the slope, Gila Jack Shadmer recognized his follower, saw that it was not the beefy form of Curly Bardoo.

A pinpoint of light winked from Shadmer's outstretched arm, and a bullet whined like a bee in flight as it passed Sidlaw's head. An instant later the sharp report of a gunshot reached the cowboy's ears above the rush of wind and the hammering of his own mount's hoofs.

With a wild oath, Gila Jack Shadmer wheeled his bronc and spurred in the direction of the paloverde which littered the hillside.

The Phantom Sheriff held his fire, knowing that to shoot would mean almost sure death for Marie Clawson.

Shadmer spurred for fresh speed. Then, with a squeal of pain the double-laden horse went down, its hoofs skidding on a rocky bench.

Sidlaw held his breath in horror as he saw the two riders flung from saddle like catapulted dummies—Marie Clawson and Shadmer.

The girl landed rolling and sprawled motionless

alongside a bubble-pitted lava boulder. But Gila Jack Shadmer bounced to his feet apparently uninjured, fanning his six-gun hammer.

Slugs burned the air around Sidlaw's body, and then he felt Curly Bardoo's horse jolted in midstride as a .32 bullet struck it.

The bronc lurched to a halt and fell. Sidlaw kicked free of the stirrups and hobbled to one side, his wounded leg making him feel faint.

Gila Jack Shadmer fired again, saw the Phantom Sheriff pitch on his face alongside Bardoo's slain horse.

Shadmer hesitated. Unhorsed, the fugitive killer knew he would have to hide quickly lest he be discovered by a pursuing posse from Smoketree.

But while there was a chance that life remained in Spook Sidlaw's motionless form, Gila Jack Shadmer did not intend to deny himself his final revenge on the Wyoming waddy who had driven him away from his outlaw empire.

Reloading his smoking Colt from ammunition in the saddlebags of his crippled horse, Gila Jack Shadmer stalked forward.

Then he glanced sideways as a movement attracted him. It was Marie Clawson, sitting up with a low moan, a hand to her head.

"I might as well make it a clean job an' finish you, too, you she-cougar!" snarled the gambler, levelling his Colt .32 at the girl's head. "You're Clawson's whelp, an'—"

With a supreme effort, the Phantom Sheriff forced his right arm to move, at the same time choking out a warning yell.

Shadmer whirled around at the cry in time to see Sidlaw prop himself off the ground with one elbow, levelling a .45 as he did so.

The two enemies fired together, the thunderclap of their shots blending as one.

Gila Jack Shadmer's bullet thudded into the lawman's hip which was already drenched with crimson and numb from the effects of the bullet lodged deep inside muscle and sinew.

Sidlaw's consciousness was smothered behind a red veil of insensibility, so that he did not see his own single shot punch an ugly hole in the center of Shadmer's forehead.

Sidlaw slumped in a faint even as the Smoketree killer buckled at the knees, the fuming Colt sagging out of his fingers.

Then Shadmer's tottering body pitched sideways, death-glazed eyes staring sightlessly at the moon.

Daylight was streaming through the curtains of Dr. Frazer's bedroom window when Spook Sidlaw opened his eyes to find himself comfortable in a white-sheeted bed.

Outdoors he could hear his coroner friend speaking to the little crowd of Smoketree citizens and cowhands from neighboring ranches, who

284

had spent the entire night watching the flames consume their courthouse.

"Yeah, I ain't spoofin' yuh—young Sidlaw will pull through O.K.!" Frazer assured the throng. "I probed three bullets out o' him—one from his side an' two from his laig. But, inside a few weeks, he'll be out an' around, I'm stakin' my rep as a doctor on that!"

Sidlaw turned his head on the cool pillow to see Marie Clawson seated at his bedside, her own head turbaned in bandages, one arm taped and splinted.

"Just go back to sleep, Spook!" the girl advised him, stealing a hand into his. "I'm all right—just bruised up some from that tumble I took. Can't you hear the town's celebrating outside? You've tamed Smoketree, Spook, and they want you to run for sheriff—to fill dad's job when you're well again. I'm so proud I feel like—well—"

The Phantom Sheriff grinned weakly.

"I jest wish—your brother Freddie—could be here now, Marie!" he whispered. "He'd 'a' prob'ly finished the job quicker'n me. But anyhow, I've fulfilled my promise to him, I reckon. An' now I kin give you back his badge, like I told you I would. Only I was wonderin'—"

"Yes, Spook?"

The girl turned her head to motion Dr. Frazer to leave, even as the grinning cow-town doctor peeped through the doorway to see how his patient was faring. The two exchanged winks, and Frazer eased the door shut.

"You were wondering, Spook—"

Sidlaw swallowed hard.

"That badge o' the Phantom Sheriff—it's made o' pure gold."

"Yes, Spook?"

"I jest wondered—mebbe Freddie would be pleased if we melted it down an' had a jeweler make a ring out of it—you think so?"

"Yes, Spook."

The waddy from Wyoming, who had ended Smoketree's reign of terror and had faced blazing guns without flinching, now found his face beaded with nervous sweat.

"Well . . . would you object . . . don't you think a jeweler . . . that is, we could make the Phantom Sheriff's star into a *weddin'* ring perty easy, Marie. Would you—"

"*Yes,* Spook!"